Imagining ISABEL

OMAR S. CASTAÑEDA

Also by Omar S. Castañeda

Imagining ISABEL

OMAR S. CASTAÑEDA

Lodestar Books

DUTTON   NEW YORK

Library of Congress Cataloging-in-Publication Data

Castañeda, Omar S., 1954–
    Imagining Isabel/Omar S. Castañeda.—1st ed.
        p.   cm.
    Sequel to: Among the volcanoes.
    Summary: Isabel, a newly married sixteen-year-old who lives in a traditional Mayan village, is invited to join a government-run teacher training program, and is thrown into the turbulent political reality of contemporary Guatemala.
    ISBN 0-525-67431-4
    [1. Mayas—Fiction.   2. Indians of Central America—Guatemala—Fiction.   3. Guatemala—Fiction.]   I. Title.
    PZ7.C26859Im   1994
[Fic]—dc20   93-50593
                                                                                                    CIP
                                                                                                    AC

Published in the United States by Lodestar Books,
an affiliate of Dutton Children's Books,
a division of Penguin Books USA Inc.,
375 Hudson Street, New York, New York 10014

Published simultaneously in Canada
by McClelland & Stewart, Toronto

Editor: Rosemary Brosnan   Designer: Marilyn Granald

Printed in the U.S.A.   First Edition
10   9   8   7   6   5   4   3   2   1

To the slain and wounded heroes of the Massacre of Santiago Atitlán, 2 December 1990; and to the more than 220,000 slain or disappeared since the 1954 coup in Guatemala.

Special thanks to Amy Walthall, who urged me to do a sequel; to Shirley Guess, for very helpful commentary; and to Rosemary Brosnan, for her superb editing, continued support, and patience.

Special thanks also to my grandmother, Sara Calderón, and to my aunt, Eugenia Méndez Duarte.

Nohol

One

Isabel gathered in the soft cloth, cradled it against her breasts, and allowed herself the luxuriant pleasure of receiving from her mother the sacred bundle given from mother to daughter for generations past. It was a swaddled thing, secret, once brightly colored, soft, murmurous with significance . . . and now it was hers.

Manuela reached out and pulled Isabel into an embrace, gritting her teeth against the wave of pain in her swollen joints. She kissed her daughter's cheek as their bodies pressed the bundle between them.

Isabel's eyes moistened with a flush of excitement.

Manuela stroked her face with great maternal love. "I'm very happy for you."

"I know," Isabel said. She daubed at her eyes. "I know."

"Lucas is a fine man. He'll be a fine husband." Manuela grimaced against her pain. "And you will be the best of wives."

The bundle in Isabel's arms felt even more like a cradled child, sleepy and immobile. "Thank you, Mother."

For a second Isabel thought that she should open the bundle with her mother there in front of her, but then she remembered that it was to be a private event in which she slowly, reverently unfolded the sacred cloth to find the hidden items placed within like fragile eggs by her mother, grandmother, great-grandmother, and still further back to women Isabel could not even imagine, but who had left in the cloth their unique legacy. Perhaps these distant women had each left something utterly common—a gray stone, a blue button—but because it had coursed through the succession of women like blood through the veins of generations, it would be imbued with something far more powerful than could be seen on the surface.

"This is for us alone," Manuela said. Her hands arched over the bundle.

"I'll guard it," Isabel assured her.

Manuela whispered, "Go, then."

Isabel grinned brightly, both out of love for her mother and with an eagerness to open the cloth she had known about for years but had always been denied access to. She had known since the age of three or four that it would take her marriage to discover what lay hidden within. It was not so long ago that she was certain she would never have this moment of discovery. Yet Isabel wanted now more than ever to see if she could identify the particular token left by her mother. She was sure that it would be radiant, as if lighted within by Manuela's unmistakable spirit . . . perhaps more so now that her mother was ill, as if to bring back for a moment her essence before the debilitating sickness turned her into a stick of a woman confined to bed for most of the day.

Manuela gently pushed Isabel's shoulders. "Go," she repeated, her voice high and light, full of sympathy for her daughter, who was finally arriving where the sky settled to earth and who no longer soared crazily.

Isabel turned and left. Behind her, Manuela blew out the candles arranged on their home altar for this bequeathing. She covered smoking incense pots and removed the blood-spotted fabric on the upper board of the altar. She swept aside the pine needles covering the stone faces below the board and slowly returned the altar to its state before the premarriage ceremony.

Up past Coxulun's coffee trees, Isabel moved onto the narrow paths between tall stalks of corn. An unseen black bird questioned the air with its metal-shearing song.

"Hey!" Loti Cotzal called to her.

Isabel waved without pausing, waved while barely noticing who it was who spoke to her from across the way.

"How is Lucas?"

But Isabel pretended not to hear. Farther on, she forked to the left and up along a black sand path, which led to a shallow cave. At the entrance, Isabel gathered her breath. She had been walking faster than she thought: Her heart raced; her chest heaved with breathing. She slowly settled back into her body.

Above the oblong entrance, madronna roots and branches twisted into a thatch of dark leaves, reddish brown bark, hoary brush. A debarked root peeked whitely through the gathered stone at the apex. Up and down the walls, rock formations overlapped one another to create vertical folds, sharp lines and angles where granite buckled into diorite, one igneous rock into another. She entered slowly, listening, for several meters; then the tunnel opened into a wide room. At the end of this room, two small paths arched outward in opposite directions. Isabel continued forward to the end of the swath of light that filtered through from the outside like a luminous carpet. She knelt. In that veiled and chiaroscuro light, she could barely make out tiny pockets in the chamber walls where others had come for their own prayers. Her nose pieced out the strong scent of green pine needles cushioning the ground. The whole sanctuary smelled of earth and forest, of moisture, of pungent life.

Isabel carefully placed the bundle on the ground before her. She gestured reverently in the four directions, finishing west, away from the lighted entrance and into the uncertain darkness of the cave. She stood and fished out a pack of matches from the waist-folds of her skirt. She searched along the walls and lit twenty candles tucked away on small shelves.

And then, with her heart beating fast, she slowly unfolded the bundle. Each unfolding made her heart *thrum* with expectation. Yet not until she had unfurled the bundle nearly a meter did the first token appear: a dried twig the length of her thumb. She held it close to her nose, inspected it, but it seemed the most boring of twigs. She replaced it on the unrolling mat. Next was a shard of pottery with the broken figure of a pregnant woman, and instantly, Isabel imagined her grandmother picking out a secret token to leave for Manuela. Isabel did not understand exactly what it meant, could not understand, but what she knew was that the token *did* mean. That was what was important. That was sufficient. And just as the broken shard meant something, so the lowly twig carried something powerful and specific to the daughter it was intended for. Later daughters, like Isabel, received from it not the particular message, but the larger message: that there was in this family a tapestry of women whose separate threads went further back than individual memory could go, yet whose combined pattern wove together past and present and future.

Isabel turned each token over in her hands as she uncovered it. She searched within the colors in stone, the chipped bone, the pottery, the sticks and glass, the seeds and swatches of cloth, to feel from them some image or clue as to the possible shape of well-wishing sent from mother to daughter. She felt happiness like a small creature chuckling in her throat. There were eleven tokens. Each made her body tingle exquisitely. At the end, she scooped as many tokens as she could into her palms and laughed out loud.

Suddenly, Isabel saw a tiny star silvering in the cloth. It was the sort dentists used to decorate teeth in the towns of Santiago Atitlán and San Lucas Tolimán. Isabel pinched free the star and turned it in her palm. It snagged the flickering candlelight. The little animal of laughter burst from her again, and she gripped the small star in her fist. She understood that *this* was her mother's gift. Isabel never would have imagined that her mother would give her such a thing. Her mother's irony surprised her. It was a sign of victory over a variety of stars: over the vain plotting of Isabel's deceitful friend Teresa, and over Isabel's own strange ambitions and ambiguous feelings. She understood that her mother would also think of it as a sign of obtaining a husband, of setting right the many constellations that

5

made up Isabel's life. Her mother had surely meant to make an emblem for the now proper reading of Isabel's stars. It was her mother's strong approval of Lucas, of the marriage, and of her daughter.

A soft scurrying made her turn to look. She saw beads of moisture trickling down the wall to pool in a small shelf that held one of the candles. The tiny rivulets hissed, quiet as a cavern lizard. Water in the first pool bulged and separated, then scurried down to the next small shelf. Beneath the second shelf, another minuscule pool waited to catch what water might break free and find that particular level to come to rest.

Isabel clutched the star tightly in her palm.

Lucas stood nervously before Isabel, struggling within himself to find the words to tell her that she was what made him unable to eat or sleep or think.

They stood in Isabel's home, playing a secret game of seeking fingers, entwining fingers, fingers searching for a hold, trying to grasp so that their hands would not separate now or later no matter what misfortunes overtook them. Around them, their two families stood, barefoot, wearing torn clothing, filling the room with the odors of the field and of wood fires, of hard work.

Lucas chuckled nervously at even this small and modest ceremony. He gazed at her round face, deep black eyes, her cheeks. "I love you," he tried to say in a soulful whisper. Instead, his voice croaked and rattled.

Isabel blushed with the knowledge that their two families were watching and listening. She squeezed Lucas's hand. "I love you, too." She would have preferred a marriage with just her and Lucas. Perhaps she would have allowed her mother to be present, bedridden and weeping dramatically from the floor, and her father, of course. Perhaps her brothers, José and Diego, and her sister, Marcelina. And she would have to have Lucas's parents. And his grandparents. She grinned at Lucas.

Eziquel Coxol, the *sanjorín*, stepped back inside the hut from going to the bathroom outside and maneuvered the couple so that they stood side by side. He brought their near hands together and draped a red sash over their wrists. Eziquel Coxol's voice grew resonant with the solemnity of prayer as he began:

O, Lord, *Dios*, Giver of Light,
Bearer and Engenderer, let these two
continue, let these two just go along
with their lives untroubled and unmolested,
without misfortune, as they travel on their way.
Help them, O Mother, O Father, beget a home, a field,
where they may plant, where they may sow,
nourishers and brighteners for you,
O, *K'ux Kah*, O *K'ux Uleu*,
Heart of Heaven, Heart of Earth.

Eziquel Coxol picked up the dangling ends of the red sash and loosely wrapped them around the joined wrists of the couple. He continued in prayer as he methodically looped each end.

Isabel barely listened to the meaning of the *sanjorín*'s words, she was so caught up in their incantatory rhythms, the incense burning along the wall, the heat, the closeness of Lucas, the certainty of it all after so many months of near-paralyzing uncertainty over marriage and over her desire to be a teacher. Now her life seemed so easy to imagine. Lucas's solid body felt like a house beam as she became increasingly light-

7

headed, almost silly with happiness and amazement. She leaned against him; he rubbed her back nearly imperceptibly.

When the *sanjorín* finished, the couple embraced. Alfredo patted Lucas on the shoulder. Demetrio Choy, Lucas's father, kissed Isabel. Beti Choy kissed her new daughter-in-law. José and Diego shifted forward to congratulate the newlyweds. Little Marcelina desperately hugged Isabel's leg.

"Let your sister go," Manuela said. She waved an uncertain hand from her mat on the floor.

Isabel separated from Lucas and Marcelina and knelt by her mother.

Manuela placed her hand against her daughter's face. Her rough fingers stroked back Isabel's hair. "So . . . there you have it."

Isabel watched the line of her mother's mouth crinkle into a smile.

"Was it so difficult?"

Isabel shook her head.

The cocoon of quiet and privacy between them hung for a luxurious moment. Lucas lanced through. "Come," he said. His fingers curled into the crook of her elbow.

Isabel saw again her mother's frail body and again felt a wave of uncertainty. Marriage was what everyone wanted of her. Yet as the oldest female, she had a duty to her sister and brothers and father now that Manuela could do next to none of the daily chores. Her mother could barely move at times, even with the medicine she took too irregularly and always with a spat. The whole flood of memories about the struggle to get Manuela to Sololá and to accept medicine knotted her stomach.

How much simpler for everyone if she did not get married.

Lucas hugged Isabel from behind. He kissed her hair.

For all of them, Isabel thought, the order of the calendar, the auguries of the stars, were set and defined.

"I'm going, Mother."

"You are going," Manuela replied.

Outside, the day was bright like any other day. Cloudless, like any other day. The trees filled with birdsong, the fields with chattering hoes and snicking machetes. Girls and women, loads balanced on their heads, walked to the lake and up the pathways as on any other day. Lake Atitlán lapped gently in the vast bowl of volcanoes and surrounding hills.

They ascended behind Lucas's mother, father, and grandparents on the way to their new home. A few friends called out as they walked. Some watched with good humor. Boys laughed and jostled one another as the couple passed. Bundles of little girls watched intently, their arms looped and entwined, their small eyes peering, their heads and shoulders pressing conspiratorially together.

It was a small parade; yet Lucas's parents walked with pride before their son and new daughter. And in that space of ritual, however small in the great scheme of things, however plain, Isabel felt a happiness inside her chest and a warmth across her abdomen at imagining Lucas lying beside her.

Two

Isabel held the bright yellow paper in her hands and swallowed. The crisp letter crinkled. She pictured Lucas out on a path, machete over his shoulder, body bent forward as he plodded up the steep hills to work. She imagined him stopping and looking back as if suddenly hearing a curious noise, something like an involuntary gasp of wonder or dismay.

She reread the letter.

It was a brief note—very official—from the Commission of Education in Guatemala City, telling her that a certain Andrés Xiloj had recommended her for a unique training program, designed to educate rural students and place them back into their own villages as teachers. The commission was pleased to report that Señorita Isabel Pacay had passed the preliminary phase in a very difficult national competition.

It was signed by a man.

The precise yet genial words of the letter made it

seem as if there had not been months of problems due to the teachers' strike and the bloody actions against it. The letter's language could make one think that life in Guatemala since Maestro Xiloj's departure six months before was languorous and gentle. The letter obliterated far too much. She did not know what to think, or feel, or what to trust.

Soon after the schools had closed, the striking teachers began their marches in the capital. They stopped traffic and blocked industry to capture everyone's attention. The newspapers brimmed and spilled over with articles condemning the teachers as irresponsible and unpatriotic, as greedy individuals who were generally incompetent to begin with, or duped by the Communists. Isabel could not imagine her teachers being duped by anyone.

In the end, nearly one hundred people—teachers, students, and angry parents—had been seriously injured in the long strike. It had been worse than Maestro Xiloj had predicted when he explained it to her six months ago. There had been *desaparecidos:* people "disappeared"—kidnapped—to be tortured as guerrillas. Inevitably, international groups entered the country. Isabel remembered the quiet immediately after. It was like the deathly quiet when Volcán de Fuego suddenly erupted and smothered all the Lake Atitlán villages in gray ash. For hours, the smaller animals struggled under the suffocating ash. For weeks afterward, the silence of birds made Isabel dream that she had died and gone to the depths of Xibalbá, that nether world.

During the quiet, Isabel and the other students in Chuuí Chopaló had returned to school. The strike lasted two months. She finished the year without seeing Maestro Xiloj. No one said anything about him. No one asked whether he would return, whether he was dead, or whether he was "disappeared."

And then, in the yellow letter from the government—so like a brittle wing—Andrés Xiloj reappeared. Yet what Isabel could not know for certain was whether he had truly appeared or whether it was a deceptive ghost of him that had come in the letter. She began to doubt everything and simultaneously to imagine everything as possible. She would need one more year before she could enter a teacher training program. And how had Xiloj entered her name without her knowledge, without her signature, a letter, a statement of purpose, her I.D. number, or countless other things the government always demanded in order to make life as difficult as possible for those trying to get just a little ahead? Even the use of yellow instead of white paper was an odd thing.

The letter should have been a flash of light in her life, but instead it reminded her of all her ambivalence. Her dream of being a teacher once more gurgled up. But containing that spring was the stony certainty of marriage, of her family duties, and of her mother's illness. She had gotten it into her head that she had to undo contradictory impulses, untangle opposing urges into a straight cord of decision and action. She had thought that unless she killed ambivalent feelings it meant that she was crazy, or unfair, or wrong. Marriage had been a way to straighten things out. Now, with the letter, she understood that her dream had been deferred.

The letter reminded her that it is one thing to have unlikely dreams stored in the pockets of one's being so that even that little weight made one bend forward and take steps—although they might be small and barely noticeable—in the direction of the dream. It was a very different thing to have unlikely dreams with no weight at all, or to chop them up with fear or with the safe certainty that the dreams would never happen. The letter taunted her with possibilities. Yet she felt like scurrying backward more than she felt like leaping forward with joy. Where would she ever find the space to go off to Sololá or to another city to attend a special training program? It was simply impossible. Perhaps she might be able to do it much later, she thought. Not now. Isabel decisively flattened the letter across her chest. Her life would come to rest for now as a wife. That was enough. That was that.

Isabel turned to see what chore she might set herself to do and saw Marcelina peeking in at the door. "And how long have you been there?" Isabel demanded.

Marcelina giggled. "You're so funny."

Isabel frowned.

"Your mouth was moving, but you weren't saying anything."

"Oh!" Isabel smiled through her embarrassment.

For Marcelina, this was an invitation to enter and begin in earnest the complete investigation of everything in her older sister's new home. With one small hand passing lightly along the wall, Marcelina took in her first impression of the room: It was small, crowded with the bed and tools and whatnots strapped to one wall, baskets making a pyramid in a corner, some shelving, and a roughly hewn chest of drawers backed up to the wall on the other side of the bed. Marcelina could not believe that her sister preferred this to her old home. The only person she would be able to speak with at night would be Lucas.

"How is Mother?" Isabel asked.

Marcelina moved in to begin a closer inspection. "Oh, you know," she said without looking up.

Isabel was quite sure that she didn't know. She watched Marcelina from the center of the room, amused at her little sister's curiosity.

"Who sleeps here?" Marcelina tested the thatch matting of the bed with her arms outstretched.

"We both do."

Marcelina screwed up her face and looked back. "Really?"

"Really."

The new bed crinkled as Marcelina pushed on the blanket covering: The fresh fibers bent and snapped as they shifted their way to more permanent positions.

"So, tell me, has she had any problems?"

Marcelina made a skip and leap using the bed frame as leverage. The blanket tassels shuddered by her knees.

Isabel raised her eyebrows. "Has Mother had any problems?"

Marcelina was already engrossed by the next thing: two baskets by the bed, one filled with clothing she had never seen.

"Are you going to stop and tell me, or not?"

Marcelina stiffened and turned toward her sister.

Isabel stared back, her fists at her waist, the yellow letter fanning out from her right hip. "Well?"

"Once, maybe." She craned her neck to look up into the apex of the thatch roof. "Once," she repeated, as if finding the answer up there in the downturned pot. Marcelina then looked at her feet. "After the wedding."

"After the wedding!"

"Yes."

"After the wedding!"

Marcelina dug her hands into her armpits.

"Why didn't anyone come and tell me?"

Marcelina remained quiet.

Isabel flapped her arms and sighed. "Well, *someone* should have come."

Marcelina waited to be released.

"Someone should have come, you know."

Her sister's resigned voice sent Marcelina spinning eagerly back to her inspection. She picked up one of Lucas's belt sashes.

Isabel felt a certain sting. She didn't know if it was that Marcelina seemed incapable of forgetting the new room long enough to speak directly to her, or that no one had needed her help when Manuela was in pain, or that something of such importance had happened without her being told. Her fingers pinched more firmly the government letter. So this was marriage, she thought.

"Whose is this?" Marcelina asked. She held out a cotton nightdress with red and blue threads.

"Mine."

"It's pretty."

Isabel smiled. Lucas had thought so as well.

"And this?" Marcelina presented another piece of clothing.

"Do you have to know everything?"

Marcelina dropped the skirt and moved to the dresser. The bundle was on top. Marcelina rose on tip-toe to peer over the edge. "What's that?" And before Isabel answered, Marcelina reached for it.

"Don't!" Isabel warned.

Marcelina drew back but she remained even more captivated by the strong prohibition. "What's in it?" She looked back mischievously. "What's it for?"

"It's a gift."

"From Mother?"

"Yes."

Her fingers fiddled with the drawer knobs just below the cloth. "What's in it?"

Isabel stood firm, the letter now flattened across her chest. She did not feel like explaining. She didn't know *how* she would explain. "Things," she said lamely.

Marcelina took that tentativeness as permission to unroll the bundle.

"Don't!"

Her small fingers paused.

Isabel stepped beside her sister. "It has special things from Mother and Grandmother." She stroked Marcelina's hair. "It's just for women. Just for us. Don't worry—and don't frown like that. When you get older, you'll see everything inside. It will be yours, too."

It would have been impossible to make Marcelina more curious. "I want to see it now!"

Isabel clutched the bundle. "It's for my wedding." She turned Marcelina away. "When you get married, you'll see it. Be patient." Isabel petted Marcelina's cheek. She kissed her forehead. "I miss you."

Marcelina squirmed with pleasure.

"You're still going to talk to me, aren't you?"

"*Sí.*" It was a word drawn out to its limits, until it became more a curling sound of emotion than a "yes."

Isabel embraced Marcelina. "You miss me, don't you?"

"Yes."

"Does Mother miss me?"

"Yes."

"And Father and José and Diego?"

"*Sííííí. . . .*"

Isabel hugged Marcelina tightly. The letter from the

16

government crinkled at her younger sister's back. "I'm glad that you're going to stay here tonight."

"Me, too."

"Diego can take care of Mother by himself, can't he?"

Marcelina opened her mouth to speak.

Suddenly Lucas called from the door. "Hey! Let me in."

The two turned to see him laden with machete, hoe, hemp bag, and several long boards. He was unable to enter the house where Isabel and Marcelina clung to each other.

Isabel quickly crumpled the letter into a yellow ball and dropped it beside the wedding bundle. She then pulled the tools from Lucas's arms so that he could enter sideways through the door with the wood planks.

The wood clattered to the floor.

"Well," he said with a great sigh. "How's the little one?"

But Marcelina was already back at the dresser, peering at the crumpled yellow letter beside the neatly folded bundle.

Three

Isabel's hands leapt into flames. Yet instead of jolting awake from her dream, Isabel settled into an uneasy curiosity as her palms burned blue hot, her fingers a wavering orange-red. She seemed perfectly awake; yet she knew she was asleep. Her hands felt heavy and stiff, and strangely cool. It took all her dream strength to place her hands together, her fingers entwining, the plumes of fire winding together, enmeshing and glowing brightly. Lucas slept beside her. He didn't move. She, on the other hand, *wanted* to move. She wanted to rise out of bed and use her hands like a torch to guide her through the terrible darkness outside. Now she was aware that there *was* something out there.

Part of her wanted to hurry out and find that thing—whatever it might be—which appeared to be past her new home, down the road, and nearer to the lake. Another part of her wanted only to rest, to accept that the darkness would always exist, and that there was no need to worry.

She tried to relax, to accept the darkness, the thing lurking beyond, the beautiful flames. Her muscles slackened and, without another thought, she was on her feet and walking toward the door. As soon as the calm overcame her, a spark of light flew from her fingers and spiraled away. It disappeared into the infinite blackness before her like a red-shifting star that twinkles out when looked at directly.

When Isabel awoke, she looked at her hands and dreamily searched between her fingers.

Lucas propped himself on one elbow. "What are you doing?"

Still foggy with sleep and languorous with her dream, Isabel said, "Seeing what fire my hands have."

Lucas stared dumbly for a second, and then he chuckled. "You're still asleep, aren't you?"

"Yes," she said. "No. I mean, no. I'm not asleep." Already the dream was washing away under so much thought and words and her waking to the tangible world. Her vision leaked through the crannies of reality.

Lucas hugged her and, without knowing, wrung what remained of the strange dream from her conscious mind. Isabel fully awakened to the need to get to morning chores. She planted her feet on the ground.

She stirred Marcelina and told her to gather eggs. When Marcelina finished, she was to help make tortillas. Marcelina scampered up from the sleeping mat, her fists grinding away into her eyes. Isabel went to the cooking hut to see if she would have to fetch water right away or if she could wait until after breakfast.

Fortunately, there was enough to hold them, so long as no one used too much to wash or drink before they all ate. She recalled her father getting up in the mornings after a night of celebration and splashing great handfuls of water onto his face and neck, guzzling water from the urn until there was nothing left. A huge moan and sigh would escape his lips, sounds that awakened anyone not already alert and signaled to the others that he would be working extra hard to repent for his aching head and parched throat. Isabel's two brothers would know that they, too, would have to work extra hard just to keep up with their father's sense of guilt. However, she would be the one to go down to the lake with the heavy urn and the one to make the tortillas and coffee. And the one to make breakfast. Isabel thanked K'ux Kah that Lucas rarely drank, unlike so many men in Chuuí Chopaló. She understood that Tzutujil men sometimes drank to forget the world, which treated them not like men, but as stupid and inferior Indians, or which presented them with so much danger that drinking was the only way to obliterate the tension and to pretend that they could say whatever it was they wanted to say.

Isabel poked the embers among the three stones of the earth and got a small flame to squirm up from the ashes. Dried corn leaves and small twigs got the fire going well enough for larger pieces of wood to be wedged in. She scooped soaked corn onto her *metate* and began rolling the grinding stone across the softened kernels to make cornmeal. She mentally guessed that she would be able to grind a pound of *masa* for the tortilla dough before the others entered. She could hear Marcelina scurrying among the huts of the compound to find eggs, awakening Lucas's parents in one hut and his grandparents in another. Slowly, everyone would come awake. The women would be the first to begin chores, making preparations for their men, or going to the kitchen hut where Isabel worked to see how things were progressing. Dutifully, Isabel began before all the others. She did not want the disapproval of the older women. The ordering and reckoning of proper behavior was done through glances and nods and indirect admonishments, never through the overt words men used to tell women exactly when and where they did something wrong. The women would sit with her and help make tortillas only after she had begun. It was her office to get the embers going, to start the coffee brewing, to fetch water, to begin grinding corn for tortillas if necessary, to warm yesterday's tortillas if there were any, and to begin the clap clap of dough.

A flash of skirt appeared at the door, then a foot and leg, then the rest of the skirt, and Beti Choy with her broad face and set eyes. "Morning," she said, and squatted by the stones.

"*Buenos.*"

Lucas's mother fingered a length of wood. She probed the embers with mild interest, then tossed the stick into the fire and dusted off her hands. "All set," she proclaimed.

"Thank you, Doña Beti."

The older woman poured water for herself and sat beside Isabel. Her hands curled around the small clay cup.

"Did you sleep well?" Isabel asked. She thought she might be able to tell of her dream.

"Yes."

Beti stared sleepily into space, perhaps considering the dreams of her own sleep, and savoring them instead

21

of the dry air of the hut or the idle chatter of her daughter-in-law.

Isabel turned her attention back to the grinding rock and did not speak. She could hear Marcelina outside rummaging in the clumps of grass by the huts. The hacking morning cough of Grandmother leapfrogged across the open space between huts, through the loose cornstalk lashings of the kitchen hut walls, and into the quiet room that slowly filled with blue smoke. Isabel pulled free a small ball of dough and clapped it flatter and rounder.

Not the coughing or the shifting of weight on straw beds, not the slurping of water or the groaning of those coming awake, transfixed Isabel, but the sharp cry of anguish lurching in from the space outside their small clutch of huts. Isabel's hands stopped in midair, the *masa* pancaked against one palm. Even before she identified that sound, she had a foreboding that jerked her to her feet. The tortilla flapped to the dirt.

"What is it?" Beti asked.

"She's dead." Her voice was flat, numb. She stared at the cup of water in Beti's hand and saw not the half-filled cup, but a cup overflowing with water.

Then Diego's gray voice came clearly into the hut, rousing all of them to the unfortunate reality coming urgently up from the lake. Isabel, however, did not imagine her mother, capturing her in the mind as if to seal in place the way she ought to be remembered; instead, Isabel shuffled through different scenarios of the way Diego may have found Manuela. Isabel imagined Diego awakening and expecting to fetch something or other for his mother while awaiting his brother's and father's return from the market in Mazatenango and, instead, finding Manuela dead. She imagined him comprehending that he was absolutely alone in the home, perhaps for the first time in his life, comprehending that he would need to find his sister.

Without crying, without feeling loss, and without guilt for not crying, she went out to meet Diego.

Down at the home, neighbors filled the yard and pressed in against the hut, all of them whispering in their hushed, murmurous voices. No one dared affront the spirit of the family or of the dead by entering the home, but they wound around one another to take turns by the door. A pathway opened for Isabel and Diego and Lucas, and the three pushed into the heart of that moribund labyrinth. At the center of the concentric whispering and lamenting, Isabel found her mother, Manuela. She had not died peacefully. Isabel put her arm over Diego's shoulder.

Manuela's hands were gnarled and crooked as if she had been clawing the world to scratch loose one last bubble of breath for her cracking lungs. Her legs were caught kicking and striking out; her mouth was twisted up as if to gather the final energy to slap the face of Death. The whorled blanket and the jumbled bed mat tracked her refusal to die quietly. She had meant to wound Death as much as her mortal strength could. Yet the fact that Diego had not leapt up, that he had not known anything of this struggle between sun and moon until it was too late, proved that it was a soundless and terrible battle, a struggle without voice, without companionship, without the air to call out for anything or anyone.

"*Dios*," Isabel gasped.

From somewhere, the need to protect her brothers and sister and father dominated all other considerations, and she spoke out so that all of them would hear—even those by the fence around the yard. "No one tells my father but me. No one!"

A solemn intoning of "Of course, Isabel; it is your duty," rose up from those gathered around.

Isabel momentarily gripped her husband's hand; then she sank to her knees beside her mother. She held the cold skin of her mother's arms, then stroked upward to the clawing fingers. She cupped the stiff joints and muscles and pressed with force until the hands curved down into a quiet repose. Isabel then massaged the fear from the jagged lines of her mother's brow, and the anguish from the lips and eyes. She molded like stiff clay the skin and skeleton of her mother so that Manuela lay becalmed, hands dropping quietly at her sides, her face turned slightly, expectantly, toward the door as if to espy her husband just now coming in, just now hurrying home to cradle her one last time. This, finally, was what released a gush of emotion from inside Isabel. She cried so loudly that her grief washed over Diego and Lucas and released their own reservoirs of sadness.

The rest of the day, they anxiously waited for Alfredo and José to return from market in time for the funeral: There were severe penalties for not burying the dead within twenty-four hours. Lucas's parents had brought Marcelina down the hill later that morning, so that all of them sat with the body just as Isabel had placed it. They prayed and burned candles and hoped that Alfredo and José would return in time for a proper invocation. Lucas spoke quietly to others to see what he could arrange about making the grave, about getting Father Ordoño from Santiago, and about speaking to Eziquel Coxol. By afternoon, they all sat together, only now and then speculating that the market could

24

be slow and Alfredo and José would need to stay another day. Or that they might miss the last bus of the day. Or that those two were on their way even as they spoke.

By nightfall, when the stars sparked in the black sky, they knew that Alfredo and José would not make it in time.

"It is better this way," Lucas's grandfather said, but Isabel understood that it was not better this way. Those were words for the mouth only: empty and for the sake of making some gesture in the great impossibility of the situation. "Alfredo will know that she is finally at rest. She has found her peace, Isabel. She will no longer suffer as she did."

"Thank you, Grandfather." She bowed her head to him.

"They may yet come," Grandmother said. "We should wait for the dawn."

"Wait for the dawn," Lucas asserted.

Marcelina curled into the warm embrace of her older sister and dropped her head against Isabel's breast.

Isabel looked out the doorway and into the night. From above the weak outline of the lake and from the barely perceptible slopes of the distant hills, the night poured into her eyes. She thought that perhaps it *was* good that her mother had died in the night. The world was really mapped out in the stars and orbits of night, instead of in the illusions of daylight. Always, it was stars—not the vaster dawn—that made the sky extend far from the earth. What the dawn brought was an end to the infinite, the possible, and a clear ceiling for the earth. Her mother had gone out into the infinitely imaginable.

* * *

25

In the morning, Isabel and the others prepared the body. Outside, the *tin-tan* of a neighbor's metal drum began the funeral dirge. It was joined after many minutes by a pair of steel pipes, whistling high notes. People gathered outside as the body was prepared inside. The sweet smoke of incense wafted into the room and around the family, which busied itself with gathering flowers into Manuela's hands, wrapping a shawl around her shoulders, pushing favorite earrings into place. At one point, Eziquel Coxol appeared with two men and a quickly made pine coffin. He put copal incense into Manuela's hands before they set her inside. Lucas went out to see who would help as pallbearers. Diego and Marcelina stood stiffly against the near wall, watching like children the workings of adults. Grandmother and Isabel leaned in and out of the space around the body, laying flat this, straightening that, pressing down, maneuvering to get the flowers and funeral paraphernalia handed to them by Lucas's parents. Coxol entered this mourning dance by weaving in and out as he prayed and blessed. As his hands went up and down, Isabel and Grandmother reached back and forth. Coxol prayed to the four corners, the pitched roof, the ground. Isabel touched away a stray hair on Manuela's cold brow.

At last, they broke into the bright daylight. The people moved in and out of the slowly forming line. They crossed before and behind, threaded through and around, rethreaded themselves, until at last they had created the appropriate pattern for the funeral march: first Isabel, Lucas, Marcelina, and Diego; next the *sanjorín*, Eziquel Coxol; the four pallbearers and coffin next; then Lucas's family; then the close friends of the family; and last, the members of the community who cared to join. Manuela's friends cried into their shawls, covering their mouths and heads. Standing aside were neighbors and people everyone knew, yet who were not close friends. There were those on their way to work, and curious children, who were eager to return to their play. Up the road, Teresa, the girl with stars in her teeth, stood respectfully back as the march progressed, as the drum and pipes picked up their discordant songs.

They followed the new water line up to the center of town, past the church and school, past the soccer field and onto the path around Oro Hill and toward the road between Santiago Atitlán and San Lucas Tolimán. There, the march turned onto a small path that led a little away from where the bus between the two towns stopped. They continued through a bean field to the cemetery. From that short distance, the few adobe mausoleums brightened the grassy area in pastel blues and greens and yellows. Among these, the modest stone crosses and tall headstones appeared like gray moorings for the gaily colored tombs. And humbly hugging the earth were the stone caps, some with names, some with chiseled marks, others completely bare.

Three of Lucas's friends looked up as the drums and pipes reached them, their shovels and picks standing out like banner poles. They quickly dug at the grave until the procession reached the half-fenced cemetery; they were already deep enough into the ground for the law, but they scraped and pulled into the earth until the last minute. And when the crowd neared, they reverently stepped back to allow the procession room.

The pallbearers lowered the casket onto two ropes laid out beside the hole. Eziquel Coxol prayed and spoke out, as best he could, what Father Ordoño might have said had there been time enough for the priest to come from Santiago. It was a mixture of the traditional and the Christian. The words of the *sanjorín* enveloped them all, friends and family alike.

Isabel reached down and gathered up a handful of soil. She waited for the final words, the end of this life. As she stood mutely waiting, the chugging bus from Santiago came around the bend and into view. All of them stared at the rocking, rickety thing; then they looked to Isabel. She watched, too, as the bus stopped suddenly and as her father came screaming from the door. No one else could be dead except his wife. No one else had been perched on that threshold for so long. He came flailing through the cornfield beside the cemetery, his anguished cries snapping the quiet of the others as they stood still as corn by the upturned earth.

Isabel looked up to heaven. She looked up, beyond Oro Hill and up to Sololá, perched so impossibly far into the sky, and then back at her lunging father. The dirt leapt from her hand and into the grave.

FOUR

The casket lid closed again.

Alfredo had emptied himself of emotion until he was nothing but a shell of a man bent grotesquely over the corpse of his wife. José, too, had become hollow and quiet, so that there was little left to do but seal the casket and lower it into the grave. Alfredo insisted that he should be the one to nail down the top, but after hammering only three nails, he could not finish. His arms dropped wearily and his shoulders collapsed. Lucas took over the task while the wind worked among the standing people as if among the hollow bells of a tubular chime: Their moans and sad cries swung out; their bodies yielded to sorrow. When the last nail barked into place, four men strained against the ropes to ease the box down. Their hands portioned out inch after inch of the rope until the coffin settled firmly into place among the rocks and clay. With the ropes pulled out, the earth began to fall in earnest.

When it was all done, the family walked together, ahead of the others, back to the house near the lake. The cord of people frayed as they moved through the village: Some left by the soccer field, pulling away to meander home; others moved on by the church and school. As they continued down through the main avenue toward the lake, their friends separated like strands from the once tight braid of mourning. The demands on those interested in living were already steering them away from the honorable luxury of grief.

"I'll leave you," Lucas said at Alfredo's home. His eyes took in the whole family, united them.

Isabel hooked herself around his waist and pressed her face into his neck. "Thank you," she whispered privately.

Lucas nodded to Alfredo and went up to his house, where he would capture what work he could from the remainder of the day. His parents reminded Alfredo and his family that whatever they needed would be at their command. "Don't you worry," Beti Choy said to Isabel. "Stay here as long as you want. I will take care of what needs to be done. Look to your family."

"Thank you, Doña Beti."

"Thank you," Alfredo echoed, but he was already drawing away from them all, isolating himself.

Marcelina clung to José's hand. Diego stood near the door, as expressionless as the old cornstalks bound tightly together to make the walls.

"Well," Demetrio Choy said. "You know where I am." He and Beti left.

Alfredo turned slowly on his heels and went to the altar, where Manuela's medicinal stone head was set beneath the horizontal plank of wood. The wood was the division between the earth gods, represented by the stone face, and the celestial gods, represented by Christian saints, the Virgin Mary, and Jesus. Manuela's lancelet, which she had used to draw blood from her arm to feed the stone mouth, lay with the point resting on the lip of a ceramic cup between incense burners. He lifted the blade and ran the point harmlessly along his forearm. A faint line whitened briefly on his skin, then disappeared. He reached out and touched his finger against his wife's dried blood, which darkened the dumb and shallow mouth of the stone. His eyes suddenly blurred with tears.

Isabel stepped alongside him.

"Basta," he said. "Enough."

He dug into his bag and pulled free the money they had earned in Mazatenango. He unfurled several quetzales and handed them to Marcelina. He told her to get Quetzalteca. "The largest bottle," he said.

Isabel's hand wavered in the air, paused between wanting to stop him and knowing that she could not or should not. Marcelina caught the hesitation and looked expectantly at her older sister.

"Go," Alfredo commanded.

The two boys sank to their haunches by the walls, hunkering down as if to wait out the day until it came to its inevitable end.

Isabel looked around to see what cleaning or straightening she might do. She would keep things as they were, not allow them to disintegrate even for a moment. She leaned forward to straighten the sleeping mat her mother had used for so many months.

Alfredo, unobservant, dug again into his *morral* and pulled out a letter from the cotton pouch. "Kahíb Tukur gave this to me in Santiago."

31

Isabel stood three yards away, her hands clutched before her.

"Take it," he said.

She stared at the white envelope and did not move. "What's the matter? Take it."

Alfredo placed it into her hand. She held the envelope awkwardly, crumpling it as if she did not want to have this intrude on their mourning. She could barely move from the heaviness of the thing.

"Open it and read it," Alfredo said.

Still she did not react, except to tighten her fingers a bit more, crumple a little bit more the long white envelope.

Her father softened his voice. "It's okay, Isabel. Go ahead and read it. There's no disrespect." His chin bobbed twice.

She spread the envelope before her, eyed it, and then read aloud: " 'El Comisión de Educación. Palacio Nacional. Guatemala.' "

"National Palace," Diego said in awe.

Isabel held the envelope up to the light, then tapped one end several times. She ripped the opposite end very slowly and blew into the slit. The letter fluttered importantly. Diego smiled. José and Alfredo exchanged glances. This was the second letter to reach the family in more than two years, and these two had come some two weeks apart.

She extracted the letter and passed the envelope to Diego. She unfolded the letter and stood among them with the crisp letter up in the air like a parchment. Her mouth worked over the first sentences.

"Aloud," Alfredo said.

" 'Dear Señorita Isabel Pacay'—they don't know I'm married!—'Dear Señorita Isabel Pacay' Choy," she added. " 'We hope this letter arrives to find you well. You have our warmest greetings and sincerest wishes that you are finding the most fulfillment in all of your endeavors—' "

"So proper," José interrupted.

" 'We are pleased to inform you that you have been selected, along with several young women from the Lake Atitlán area, to enter the Teachers' Training Program to be presented in Sololá.' " She looked over the letter at her father. " 'Congratulations on your successful completion of the competition and on the future success of your studies—' "

Marcelina entered with a soft clinking of coins against the large bottle of Quetzalteca liquor.

"Ah," Alfredo said, gathering in the change and bottle. "Get me a glass." Marcelina fetched a cup and salt dish, and sliced a lime she had picked on her way.

Isabel read to herself the remainder of the letter as Alfredo poured a squat glassful of the strong liquor. He gulped it down, shook himself through the burning taste, then tempered it with a lime wedge and salt. "Continue," he said, pouring another drink.

" 'As you know, the program accepted only the best students from hamlets for the rigorous training session. It is our great hope to see Guatemala grow fat and healthy as a nation with the full potential of our young people. Only through education can we develop as a major presence within Latin America . . .' "

Alfredo gulped down another drink and poured yet a third. Isabel and her siblings looked at one another. They knew that he would soon be very drunk. He never drank so fast as he did now, nor did he ever buy so much as he had in this uncommon act.

Isabel skipped past the ornate language full of unrestrained nationalism to get at the heart of the matter. " 'Trainees will attend classes at Colegio Santa Teresita. Room and board can be provided for twenty quetzales per month—' "

"Hah!" Alfredo said, and tossed down his third cup. His mouth watered from the powerful taste. Already his eyes were glazing over, and his face reddened from the third glassful in fewer than ten minutes. He gurgled at the back of his throat. "Twenty quetzales!"

" 'However, trainees need to stay at the Santa Teresita School.' "

A strange *beerp* came from Alfredo's throat. He lifted his fourth glass and spoke Manuela's name through a sudden overflow of tears, excess saliva from the terrible alcohol, and a runny nose from his body's fight against the spiny poison. "Manuela" bubbled out from all that wetness like a pathetic sob. Then he gulped his fourth drink. "Read again," he gushed. "Read it again!"

She watched him pour the last of the bottle into the cup and hold it at arm's length. "Father," she began, but he was no longer really listening to her. Neither was he completely drunk yet. It would take a few more minutes for the large quantity to take full effect. Instead, he balanced himself to drink the last of the alcohol.

She read so as not to think about what he was doing to himself. " 'A stipend of one hundred quetzales per month will be given to those accepting the eight-week training program—' "

"Stop!" Alfredo shouted. His drink still hung in the air. He furrowed his brows and tried to discover through the invading fog whether or not he had heard correctly. "Read that again."

" 'A stipend of one hundred quetzales per month will

be given to those accepting the eight-week training program—' "

"*¡Híjole!*" he said, his eyebrows springing up with glee. He smiled hugely at José.

" 'We require that candidates send their replies—' "

"That!" he said, "is something to read again! Read it again."

"Please, Father . . ."

He swallowed the last of the liquor and bit down on a wedge of lime. His eyes closed; he hunched his shoulders and shuddered.

"Your mother would want to hear that," he said finally. "Read it again."

She gave in. " 'A stipend of one hundred quetzales per month will be given to those accepting the eight-week training program.' "

He wavered and was already unable to focus well. "What came after that?"

" 'We require that candidates send in their replies no later than three weeks from the date of this letter.' " Isabel looked at the top of the page. "By sixteen days."

Alfredo tried to pour another cupful. A small trickle ran out from the upturned bottle. He wiggled it. He raised his cup and toasted Isabel. "My daughter!" he cried out. "The teacher!" He took in the others. "Aren't you proud of your sister?"

They stared with excited yet wary expressions. They knew Alfredo would not be violent or angry, yet they did not know how he would change. Sometimes he became very funny, other times only maddeningly repetitive.

Suddenly Alfredo began to cry again. "Poor Manuela," he blubbered. He rolled the cup against his lips. "She suffered so much, Isabel. She could not sleep at night."

His voice resonated in the cup. "You don't know how much it hurt her. You don't know how much she hurt."

Isabel sat beside him. She could barely keep from crying again, seeing him this way. "Father," she whispered, but the alcohol had already short-circuited him so that he did not listen.

He draped a hand down across his face and came up sucking air. "At least she died calmly," he declared. He tried to drink from the cup again. "At least she died calmly. Not fighting like she did every night, Isabel." He glared at his daughter's face. "That's good, isn't it?"

"Don't do this," she said. "Why do you have to drink?"

He was off on his own meanderings. "She didn't see that you were going to do all right, Isabel. Like I imagined for you. She thought you would not do the right thing with Lucas and—" He shuddered from the taste of the alcohol climbing back up his throat.

The smell from him was strong. "Lie down," she said. Isabel motioned for Diego and José to help her maneuver him to the bed mat. Marcelina grew small and quiet.

"And now this honor comes for you," he said, as if there were a logical pattern to his words. "Honor, hah! How can we have honor here?" His body began to slide. "You and Lucas can go to Sol-ay," he hiccoughed. "I mean, Sol-ay." He laughed. "I mean, So-lo-lo-lá." He laughed giddily.

José reached to support him under his arms and lift him to his feet. Diego adjusted his legs and pants. When his head flopped to one side, Marcelina appeared in front of him.

"Poor Marcelinita." Alfredo suddenly straightened with inspiration. "Take Marcelina! Send the money to Lucas! You can take Marcelinita." He rubbed at his face. "Oh, he'll never accept that. Take her, Isabel. Like a *familito*, *¡tan chulito!*" He succumbed to stupid chortling. It ended abruptly with his spitting and drooling. "Bufg," he said.

"Lie down," she coaxed. She took his hands and pulled him toward the bed as the two boys guided his sprawling, stumbling weight. "Rest, Father."

"He hasn't eaten anything," José said.

"Let's eat!" Alfredo called out, taken by that new idea. "Make some food, Isabel. Get me some beans. Make tortillas for all of us, Isabel." He took one step backward and then staggered under the control of his sons. "Manuela," he muttered. His eyes grew wild and his body stiffened. And then he bent his head down and vomited by his feet.

The boys groaned. Marcelina covered her face.

"Help him to bed!" Isabel commanded. She pulled on José's arm and turned them in the proper direction. "Marcelina, get water and clean that up."

José and Diego stepped back as soon as they placed him on the mat. Alfredo moaned loudly, sickly.

Isabel crouched beside him and held his face. "Why do you do this? Why?" She looked up to see her two brothers staring with disgust at their father. Anger suddenly overcame her. "Why are you looking at him like that?" she yelled. They turned their faces down. "Don't you dare look at him like that!" She reached for the basket of rags kept by the bed mat to make clothing and patches. She pulled out a red-and-green swatch of cloth to wipe Alfredo's face. "There," she said. She stroked around his lips, under his chin. His head lolled drunkenly when she let it go. Isabel glowered at her brothers. "Go help Marcelina! Now!"

Isabel carefully daubed at his neck and over his brow. She tossed the rag to the ground and situated his head on the pillow. His body straightened as he settled into sleep.

Perhaps, Isabel thought, he will have one last night of believing his wife slept beside him. She again lifted the basket lid and, for a brief moment, she imagined the rag basket as her suitcase. She saw herself arranging her own tattered clothes within.

Xaman

Five

Alfredo spread his arms and nudged Isabel further back into the shadows of their discussion. "Now," he continued, "Marcelina needs greater care. It is too much for her to lose her mother. The boys are a little different."

"They are older," Lucas said.

"And Isabel has so many more responsibilities now that she is a wife and a daughter-in-law."

"No, Don Alfredo, she has too many responsibilities."

"After all, she must take care of her husband's wishes."

Lucas crossed his arms. "Yes," he said.

"She must obey her mother-in-law and make sure that she offers herself to the task if Father-in-law has some errand to run."

"It is anything but easy," Lucas said.

Alfredo leaned back on the stump and against the wall. "It is very difficult."

"Very difficult," Lucas echoed.

Alfredo let go a sigh. "And though the boys are older, there is her duty to them, as well."

Lucas shook his head in agreement.

"Of course," Alfredo added quickly, "I don't need anything."

"Oh, no," said Lucas.

"No, I'm an old man who has grown accustomed to taking care of himself. I'm no child, you know, who needs to be watched after."

"Certainly not," Lucas said.

"Ah, but those brothers . . ."

"They are another matter."

"Yes." Alfredo rubbed his hands between his knees. "You see the problem, then."

"I believe I see the problem."

The two men sat apart, Alfredo with his hands pressed flat together between his knees, Lucas with his hands holding his elbows. Isabel had all but disappeared against the wall. The two of them acted as if she did not exist. She tried to listen carefully to see which one was imagining a life for her that she liked.

Alfredo spoke half to himself. "I will have to pay Eziquel Coxol for his services. The stone cutter, too. And those who dug the grave."

"There's time for that," Lucas said. "They will understand. They're my friends. I don't think there is a hurry."

"Still, one should meet one's obligations."

"Of course!" Lucas said.

"As soon as possible." Alfredo shrugged. "There is never enough money."

"Never."

"And whenever we delay our debts, we only take in

41

more debts. It is a circle that tightens around our stomachs."

Lucas tightened his arms across his chest. "This is true."

"We are always obliged to find ways to make just a little more money. Just a bit here and there to meet what comes up."

"It is a sacrifice," Lucas said.

"Yes, it seems there is never an end to the sacrifices we must make for our families."

"No, Don Alfredo, it is difficult."

"In the end, in the final accounting, in the laying out of things, however, there is benefit, something to be gained."

Lucas's hands opened onto his lap. "Yes, but at what cost?"

"No, that's the issue."

"There are duties that are lost."

"No," Alfredo said resignedly, "it is very much a problem. A big problem. That's for certain."

"And then there are the grandparents."

"Oh."

"They're very traditional," Lucas whispered. "They expect things to be done in the same way they did it. They don't understand that things change."

Alfredo's hands spread out before him, palms up to the ceiling. "One wonders how they ever managed before they got such things as a daughter-in-law."

Lucas harumphed in his throat. "She has been such a help to everyone."

"She's a good daughter. Why wouldn't she be a good wife?"

"Of course."

"Well, a wife wants to be with her husband every minute of the day."

"They should be together like husband and wife," Lucas said. "Not every minute of the day. After all, there's work to be done."

"To make a living."

"Yes, to earn money," said Lucas emphatically.

Alfredo slowly nodded in agreement.

Lucas put his hands flat together and pressed them between his knees. "Money," he said helplessly. "It's difficult to get and yet we need it to survive."

Alfredo crossed his arms on his chest. "No, it seems impossible to think of a way to get any."

Early that evening, Lucas sat beside the fire and stirred the beans. His grandmother eyed him suspiciously. He poked the fire to send up a healthy chatter of flames.

"Two months isn't such a long time," he continued. "I remember you, Grandmother, telling me that you were apart from Grandfather for two years."

The old woman's graying hair was braided and coiled on top of her head. One side had slid down so that it seemed about to cascade down her shoulders. "Hmm," she answered.

Isabel looked intently into the corn *masa* she kneaded and rolled. She and Grandmother were well along in making tortillas. Now and then Grandmother wordlessly pinched out a ball from the dough Isabel prepared and clapped it flat. Lucas reached for each tortilla as she finished and situated it against the fire; he turned them frequently to avoid burning. He made a large gesture of the fact that he was helping. The two women tolerated Lucas's presence in the kitchen hut.

"And didn't Father leave my mother for—"

"Here," Grandmother said, inserting another tortilla into his hands.

Lucas placed it quickly. "I think it would be good for us to have one hundred quetzales per month."

Grandmother massaged a lump of dough into a circle. "How long have you been married?"

Lucas flattened his legs out. "It hasn't been long, has it?"

"Our corn lasts longer on the stalk," she said.

Lucas chuckled uncomfortably. He studied the tortillas and flames, searching in that heated dance for some new steps.

"Perhaps I could find someone to do my work, and then I could go to Sololá, as well."

Isabel cleared her throat.

"You would pay this person?" Grandmother questioned.

"I might find work in the city."

"You have work here."

"I suppose it doesn't seem very likely, does it?"

"Perhaps you'll find turtles in the lake," Grandmother answered.

Lucas winced at the impossibility.

Isabel grinned into her work.

"I just think," Lucas continued, "that there may be ways to do this. We shouldn't let opportunities go by without thinking about them." He jabbed at the fire.

Grandmother shook her head. "All opportunities shimmer when they first appear."

"What do you think?" Lucas asked Isabel.

She did not look up. "I don't know."

44

"One hundred quetzales is a lot of money for us."
She worked another tortilla.

"Perhaps the three of us can go," he said.

"Three?" asked Grandmother.

"With Marcelina, I mean."

"You and Marcelina and Isabel?" Grandmother stared at him with undisguised disbelief.

"Well, yes."

"And your fields?" she pointed out. "Are you going to pay one of your friends to do the work? How much will you pay?"

"I don't know!" He stood in frustration and left without another word.

Isabel watched him go. Grandmother shot a glance at her.

"I don't know," Isabel answered timidly. She checked the sides of the tortillas, turned some against the heat, removed those already done. "I don't know."

They finished in silence. Minutes later, the others entered to eat. Beti and Demetrio sat close together by the doorway. Grandfather sat across the fire from his wife. Lucas settled in against the wall, one knee raised. He still struggled with his plans. His fingers plucked and stroked as if in that unconscious activity he could kindle the appropriate words. Isabel ladled black beans onto plates and passed them to Grandmother, who then covered them with tortillas kept warm within a rag by her side. She handed the first plate to Demetrio Choy, the second to Beti. Grandfather passed them a small dish with salt and green chilies. Lucas received the third plate, Grandfather and Grandmother the next plates. Isabel served herself last and settled beside Lucas.

His eyes were already moving with plans to address

45

again the issues in his mind. Isabel pretended not to notice, but she did. She saw in his every aspect the struggle to imagine the way to make her trip happen. Yet he seemed not to care what she thought about it.

"Well," Lucas finally blurted out, "this going to Sololá is an interesting idea."

No one accepted the bait.

"A very good idea," he persisted. "Two hundred quetzales. That's a lot of money. That's more than many men make working in the fields for those same two months."

The family looked at Isabel.

"I won't accept, then," she said.

Lucas rocked back. "No! I mean that's good. Two hundred quetzales is good."

"What about my brothers and sister?" she asked.

"Of course they would have their share of it."

Isabel wilted down.

"She means," Beti said, "who is going to take care of her brothers and sister?"

Lucas scooped up a mouthful of beans.

"You have two families to care for now," Grandmother said.

"Marcelina will have to come live here," added Grandfather. "It's the only way."

Lucas gestured with a tortilla. "She can go with us to Sololá. If we stay in the school, the money won't be spent on living. I can work here and return to Sololá in the evenings. Simple."

"Perhaps," his father said, "you will spend two hundred quetzales on the bus and boat. Is there something to gain in that?"

"Perhaps the owners of the *Jucán Ya* will be generous," Lucas said around a bite of beans.

46

"The only way," Isabel inserted, "is alone." She stared at her plate. "Or if Marcelina goes with me."

"That's impossible," said Grandmother. "A woman alone in the city! Impossible!"

Yet Lucas placed his empty plate on the ground and drew closer to Isabel. "It really isn't very long at all, Isabel. I could go every week."

She felt the warmth of his body, he was so close.

"We need the money."

Isabel frowned at him.

"It would be very little time apart. Hardly any time, it would pass so quickly."

Her eyes flushed with tears.

"The money would help us, Isabel."

She scooped the remainder of her beans into her mouth.

"Well?" he asked. "It's not a bad idea."

She chewed and cried.

Lucas drew back in amazement, thinking for a brief moment that she was joking. "What?" he said. He turned uncomfortably to the others. "What? Why is she crying?" They politely did not look at Isabel or Lucas. He turned back to her. "Isn't this what you wanted? Isn't this exactly what we had trouble with before? Isn't this the promise I made to you? I don't understand. What's wrong?"

Isabel darted out the door.

Lucas gaped dumbly after her. "What did I say?" He peered questioningly back at the others. "What did I say?"

Only Beti faced him. "Too much."

The others dug deep into their food.

Lucas found her sitting on their bed with her back pressed firmly against the branches of the wall,

almost hidden in the darkness. He stood at the doorway.

"I thought this was something you wanted. I don't
understand."

"We'd be apart."

He closed the dark space between them. "It
wouldn't—"

She put her fingers against his mouth. When he
relaxed, she said, "I know this is what I wanted. It's
just . . . I'm afraid, Lucas. I don't know what will
become of me."

He chuckled, then stopped when he caught her
warning glare. "I'm sorry, but there's nothing to fear.
You'll be with other teachers in the school. You'll be
taken care of."

She huddled her fists against her chest.

"There's nothing to worry about."

She felt smaller and smaller in the darkness of the
hut. "I'm afraid. I don't want to be without you. It's
too soon."

"Maestro Xiloj would not have arranged this if he
didn't think you could do it." He stroked her. "There's
nothing to fear."

"And where is he now? Where did they get the information? I never sent it to them. Who are they?"

He stood to stretch free of the tension churning
between them. "There's no reason to worry. If you send
the letter to accept, you'll get more information." His
hands blossomed open before her. "If it's all a lie, then
you come back and nothing has changed."

"I don't know. I would have to take Marcelina. It's
all too strange."

He returned gently to her side. "I would visit. I'd go
as often as possible."

"We'd be apart, Lucas. Doesn't that matter?"

Isabel lowered her eyes and pressed herself against him. She kissed his neck. Her eyelashes brushed his earlobe, and her breathing became a small, expectant bubble close to her mouth.

Lucas touched her face. He rolled strands of her hair between his fingers. He touched and stroked her hair until his own uncertainty was combed away. He urged her face up to press his mouth against hers. And he gathered her into his arms.

Six

After all was said and done, it was Lucas who mailed the letter to the Commission of Education one week later. He took the brief letter written by Isabel—she did not want to write something long for fear that she would make some error in spelling or in grammar and thus lose the chance given to her—and carefully folded it in four parts to fit into the small, blue-green envelope. It was almost to the deadline; there were only a few days left. Lucas made the special trip by bus to Santiago Atitlán. There, in the late morning, with the fog already dissipated from the shoal reeds and shoreline brush, he ascended the hill into the busy center. Up in the square, beside the Health Center, he found the small post office.

He spoke to a ladino, a man of mixed breed, with a chubby red face, slouched over a desk bare but for two small cups just inches apart. "Do I place my letter here?" Lucas asked in Spanish.

The man lifted his head from the desk and told him that the mail would not leave until the following morning. It had already left for the day.

"But I should mail it today," Lucas said.

The reply was simple: "I'm sorry."

"Perhaps someone will take it to Panajachel," Lucas said.

But the ladino had already lost interest in him. His head drooped back to the desk top. His fingers dipped idly into the small cups.

Lucas was anxious not to have the letter delayed even another day in Santiago, particularly since there was no guarantee that the letter would make it out of town the next day, anyway. Things could move at a pace to frustrate even the mountains of the lake. He was determined to find someone traveling to Panajachel or to Sololá who would deliver it to the post office of either place. Those two towns, inundated as they were by tourists, had developed a certain efficiency. If he found someone going to the capital, even better.

Lucas entered the Restaurant Susy. He waited standing up in the blue room until the owner, Carlota, finished serving a table. She turned to him and asked in broken Tzutujil what he wanted. He said that he wished to find someone who would do him a little favor, a little task, in Sololá. She eyed him suspiciously. "Just to mail a letter," he said. "That is all. Just that."

"Juan!" she called.

Her husband came out with a cigarette in his mouth. His Tzutujil was perfect. "The only thing is to go to the docks to see who might be traveling there," he said. "Go down there. No one here is making the trip."

"By the docks, then?" Lucas asked politely.

"Yes, go to the docks and see. Perhaps someone is

51

making the trip to Sololá or Panajachel today. Perhaps someone in the Mariposa."

"There is someone in the Mariposa going today?"

"Perhaps no one is going today."

"Perhaps one of the women," Lucas said, "one of the widows."

"Yes, Doña Beatríz or one of the women may go today to Panajachel."

Lucas smiled. *"Maltioch,"* he said. "Thank you."

He descended the steep hill toward the docks where the tourist boats landed. He hugged the side of the street as he went, not wanting to bump into tourists or be caught by their unabashed picture taking. Lucas hurried as quickly as he could down to the widows' shop.

The Mariposa was crowded. Doña Beatríz gestured minutely beside two young widows to let him know that she saw him. The shoppers in this store entered and left quickly, and many seemed taken aback by the bead-work sold by the widows. One man protested that the work was exactly like jewelry he saw everywhere in San Francisco. Lucas thought that that was the purpose of the store: to sell things that Americans were accustomed to buying. Doña Beatríz patiently communicated to the stranger that the store was completely run by widows, some barely into their adolescent years. They were all, she said, reminders that death by natural causes is an infrequent luxury in Guatemala. For some, she added, crafting the designs of Roberto, the American, was the only living they could gain. Beatríz detailed all this in a voice that netted all the customers in the store and dragged them squirming up to the counter. Their wallets opened, and money spread out before her like bandages and salves and documents of pity.

Lucas watched the younger widows smile behind their shawls. They took in everything that Doña Beatríz did, how she spoke and moved in front of the tourists. These two women, the same age as Isabel, kept their arms looped together, their heads inches apart, shawls up to their necks or mouths, looking like young women should who are appropriately restrained and humble. But these women were learning how to make of their lives something centered upon the untying of foreign purse-strings, instead of making lives tied to the house and hearth, to the ways of planting, to parturition. The last straw for Lucas came when a young European woman entered with a great swirl of her skirt. The two widows moved excitedly. The self-absorbed woman directed her companion by his hand up to the counter display. There, she clapped her hands together in exaggerated glee and let go a high-pitched squeal. Lucas glanced at the ecstatic faces of the two Tzutujil women and walked out of the store.

At the end of the street, the way became dirt and grass down to the docks. There, women fetched water from the older, rickety docks, while boys and men fished along the shore and into the laguna of Santiago. Some children swam just a little further out than the women washing clothes. Wrap-around skirts and blankets dried on the grassy bank and atop large gray rocks rising from the water. These women made a gigantic tapestry of the earth, their weavings, the natural stone, the rhythms of their labor. The men who worked the tourist boats stretched out on the grass, smoking cigarettes or talking around long-stemmed grasses.

Lucas ambled down by the boards, feeling his irritation growing and getting more anxious to return to Chuuí Chopaló with his postal mission accomplished. He searched out the faces among the docks and grassy places. Three young men sat chortling atop a boulder directly in front of the *Huitzitzil*. Lucas stared at them long enough for the young men to stare back with a clear challenge. One was the cousin of his friend María. Lucas was sure of it, though his clothing was not at all what he would have expected. Suddenly, the man recognized Lucas and called out to him in Spanish.

"Días," Lucas replied.

Gaspar wore Nike shoes and blue jeans cinched at the waist by a leather belt woven through with Guatemalan cloth. He wore a shirt depicting a man bursting into flames. Black and red letters dripped like blood in the words "Ozzy Eats It Raw."

"How are you?" Lucas asked in Tzutujil. "How is your family?"

"Are you going to Panajachel?" asked Gaspar in Spanish.

"No," he answered. In Tzutujil, Lucas said, "I am on an errand."

Gaspar's friends shifted on the rock. One of them extracted a cigarette and lit it.

"On an errand," Gaspar repeated in Spanish. "Oh."

"Sí," Lucas said.

Gaspar took a cigarette, offered it to Lucas.

"Gracias, no."

They both looked out over the grass at the women washing clothes. A little boy leaped naked from rocks and into the water.

"There's an errand I need to do in Panajachel,"

Lucas continued in Spanish. "I need to mail a letter in the post office of Panajachel."

Gaspar's friends looked over with affected boredom.

"I need to put this letter in the post office."

"Oh," Gaspar said. He bent down and wiped his shoe top. "The *Huitzitzil* will leave soon."

"The post office in Sololá would be good, too. Either one is good, I think."

One of the friends placed his arm over Gaspar's shoulder and jostled him. "He wants someone to mail the letter for him." He jerked his chin at Lucas. "Is that what you want?"

Lucas felt uncomfortable with the directness. "Are you from the capital?" he asked.

The man laughed. He swept his other arm over the other friend's shoulder and pulled him so the three of them squeezed close. "Yes, we're from the capital. Isn't that right, Moro?" The other friend snickered.

"You're going to the capital?"

Gaspar shook his head. His companions chuckled.

"To Sololá, then?"

Martín, the brusque one, waved at Lucas. "No, man, we don't have time to take your letter to the post office. Unless you want to pay us. You want to pay us something to do your errand?"

Lucas looked questioningly at Gaspar, who grimaced with discomfort.

"Pay you?" Lucas asked.

"*Sí, mon.*"

Gaspar stood away from his friends and spoke to Lucas in Tzutujil. "Look, I don't think we have time to do this favor for you. We have errands to do. They will keep us too busy. If it weren't for that, I—"

Martín yanked Gaspar's sleeve. "Come on! The boat's leaving."

The boys of the *Huitzitzil* unloosed the boat and held the ropes in hand. The motor rattled up; the horn blasted three times.

"Come on," Martín said again. He faced Gaspar and Lucas, one arm hooked over Moro's shoulder. When Gaspar didn't move, he clicked his tongue, and he and Moro turned up onto the dock.

"If I had time," Gaspar said in Tzutujil, "I would do this for you. I'm sorry."

Lucas gazed down at Gaspar's shoes and up at his clothes. Lucas could hardly believe that this person was from Chuuí Chopaló. Worse, he could hardly believe that he was in such a needy situation where he would have to trust someone like him.

"I'm sorry," Gaspar said, and walked up the dock.

Lucas followed him. "It won't take long," he pleaded.

Martín and Moro had already climbed onto the top of the boat, where a few tourists with bandannas around their heads stretched against their large backpacks. They sat beside a woman in halter top and shorts, talking animatedly and barely interested in Gaspar's progress up the dock.

"Are you with them, Gaspar?" Lucas asked, still not believing.

Gaspar stopped. He looked at his friends, then back at Lucas. He moved his shoulders as if wriggling free of something binding him, containing him.

"Perhaps you'll mail the letter for me," Lucas tried again. "At Pana, it doesn't matter. Or Sololá. That's better, but it doesn't matter."

Gaspar stepped aboard. "I'm sorry," he said again. "If I had more time, I would. Of course I would."

The crew threw the ropes on deck and helped the last passengers on. Lucas held the letter limply in his hand and felt a burning in his chest. The boat edged slowly back, and suddenly Gaspar snatched the letter. "Okay," he said. "Don't worry."

But Lucas did. Before he knew what he had done, Lucas stepped across the open space between boat and ground and found himself clinging to the white metal poles of the gangway. He stood very still, hanging tightly to pole and letter—fighting the incomprehensible pull of Isabel's letter—and wondered how in heaven he would get off this boat slipping away toward the north shore of the lake.

Seven

Marcelina moved eagerly to her sister's side.

Isabel had the old rag basket opened on the bed. She looked down and could not help but recall her mother's casket. She quickly wrapped an arm around Marcelina's shoulder and hugged her close. "I don't believe this is happening," she said into the basket, half expecting the words to drop down, then rise up in strange echoes.

Marcelina peered down, too, then she twisted suddenly away in a little prance and squeal.

Isabel laughed. She fell onto the bed and pulled Marcelina into her arms. Marcelina burrowed happily. They got silly fast, wriggling and tickling until they were both enjoying the playfulness and comfort of each other's bodies. Isabel kissed Marcelina on the forehead. She held Marcelina's face in her hands and looked into her brown eyes. "I love you, Marcelina," she said. "I'm so glad you're coming with me." She kissed her face. "My little *tzunún*, my little hummingbird."

Marcelina buried her cheek in Isabel's neck.

"You'll be my helper, won't you?"

Marcelina mewled a "yes." She drew her hand up and let it rest between her sister's breasts, large in comparison to her own childlike ones. She inspected her older sister's chin and lips. She reached up and, with uninhibited curiosity, outlined her thick lips, her nose, brow, and down again to her breasts. She cupped Isabel's right breast in her small hand, calculating, weighing, then she thrust herself flat on her back to feel her own chest. Her lips pursed when she arched to make her bosom swell.

Isabel chuckled. She took hold of Marcelina's hand and pulled her up. "Let's pack."

There wasn't much, but every little bit had to be ceremoniously held up, judged worthy, and carefully folded and tucked in. Isabel held out her *huipil*. Marcelina chanted, "Oh, yes!"

"Are you sure, little one?"

And Marcelina replied, "Oh, yes!" And then they folded neatly and smoothly the chosen blouse.

Beti heard the two having so much fun that she entered. She sat on the edge of the bed. Marcelina restrained herself in Beti's presence. It was her compound, really. While the men talked at length and gave orders, the women communicated in quiet gestures, small motions, discrete words, conveying, it seemed, far more than the men, and understanding between them far more. Marcelina shrank a little away, but Beti smiled encouragingly. In minutes, Grandmother came in, too. She sat against the wall.

"So, Lucas will come back tonight?" Beti observed.

"Yes, Mother-in-law." Isabel could not imagine what it would feel like to not have him lying beside her. But

his snoring also made the thought of his absence somewhat pleasurable.

"No need to take too much," Beti said.

"No, Mother-in-law." Isabel held up everything so
that there would be no mystery as to what she took
northward and upward to Sololá.

Marcelina tightly rolled a handful of menstruation
rags and wedged them against the sides of the basket so
that the contents would not shift too much.

Grandmother sat quietly, moving only in that she frequently passed her hard, wrinkled hand down over her
face. Isabel was grateful for the silent prayers.

"And when will you return for the first time?"

"When Lucas comes to bring me back, Mother-in-
law."

"I see," Beti said, visibly pleased that Isabel had
answered so properly: She at once had said that as
soon as it was possible she would return and that she
would remain obedient to the wishes of her husband.
"Perhaps it won't be so bad, this going."

"Thank you," Isabel said. She indicated Marcelina.
"I will have my helper, Mother-in-law."

Beti smiled.

Grandmother's hand slid down across her brow, her
eyes, her nose and mouth, then curled under her chin
to make another pass down her face.

Lucas peered in the doorway, opened his mouth as if
to speak, then saw the configuration of women. "I'll
come back," he said, and left.

Isabel glanced at Beti.

"I suppose the money will be good."

"Perhaps," Isabel answered hopefully.

"This will not be a long stay."

"No."

60

"And it is only across the lake, after all."

"Very near," Isabel said.

Marcelina pinched the barest hold on Isabel's skirt as she rocked her bottom against the bed frame. Isabel stood alert. The packing was finished.

Beti peered around the room. "All right," she declared. She scribbled a finger through the air. "You had better go take care of her things now."

"Yes, Mother-in-law." Isabel took Marcelina's hand from her skirt. "Come. We'll go down to the house."

Beside them, Grandmother twisted and creaked to her feet.

Beti remained seated.

"I'll find Lucas," said Isabel.

Beti nodded, and the others left her in the shadowed room.

Several hours later, Lucas, Isabel, and Marcelina stepped from the bus and walked down to the docks of Santiago Atitlán. It had been an uneventful ride, the bus nearly empty on its last leg between San Lucas and Santiago. The old Blue Bird bus shrugged and nodded along the pitted road and made its slow way out. Before that, their good-byes had been quiet. Alfredo and his sons had said little to her or to Marcelina. Time was a sphere where humans walked in four directions, but always, always, there was a coming home. In the face of that, not much could be said except quick well-wishing and prayers so that the way would be bright and without danger in front or from behind.

They waited for half an hour on the grassy banks of the lake until the boatmen began to call people on. Isabel settled into a seat in the cabin area behind a group of women from Santiago. Marcelina sat beside her against the window, and Lucas positioned himself by the aisle as a kind of protection. Marcelina constantly mouthed the hem of her shawl and concealed part of her face. Her small eyes darted sideways and gathered in all that came before her. Lucas sat very rigidly, his hands folded above the seat in front of him.

Isabel watched the parade of people onto the dock to her left. She recalled the last time she had made this trip. That time, when Lucas had been so angry with her that they did not speak, it was to take her mother to a doctor in Sololá. She remembered how her family had chuckled over the foreigners. They sometimes did not know whether a foreigner was male or female, they dressed so strangely. Some men would wear Guatemalan clothing made for women, and their women dressed like men or they wore next to nothing at all. This group seemed to be made up mostly of men and women who liked to wear as little as possible. The women wore bathing suits that were no more than bras and underwear; the men wore bathing suit bottoms and loose, flapping shirts or no shirts. These women made Isabel feel beautiful; they had so much ugly leg and thigh and stomach and underarm and pale flesh standing out for anyone to see. Isabel looked over at Lucas, who stared ahead.

Two foreign women pressed their way to the front cabin seats and settled in with a flurry of backpacks and loud words. They heaved up their feet, planting them against the forward cabin wall, long legs angling into full view, and each lit a cigarette. Large blue clouds issued from their mouths. Those behind them silently opened a window. Each time they pulled on the cigarettes, their many silver bracelets jangled up and down their thin arms.

62

Lucas beamed at Isabel.

Isabel cocked her head. "It is beyond knowing," she said.

"Listen," he whispered. "They're speaking Spanish."

It was true: The Spanish was very fast, a chattering, the words crunched in their toothy mouths, then spit out with a lisping tongue.

"Spaniards," Lucas said.

Marcelina peered mousily from behind her shawl.

Isabel recalled that Maestro Xiloj liked to tease about the Spaniards' way of speaking—it was his way of mildly attacking the prestige of Spanish Spanish over Guatemalan Spanish. He said that they talked as if they were emptying their minds directly into their mouths as they thought. They do not know that they have time, he would say. That is why they move and speak without hesitation, even before they know what it is they are doing or what the effect will be. They think that at any moment all will be lost.

Isabel smiled to herself, thinking of the mischievous laughter his speech would elicit. "But look at them," he would add. "In fewer than five hundred years, they have been transformed, while we, well, we are still here among the rocks and trees, among the cocksfoot as before, moving so patiently that we seem to have disappeared to those quickly darting eyes."

Lucas cast a glance at Marcelina, then nestled his words close in for Isabel. "I'll miss you."

She felt his body loosen, take on the weight of affection for her.

"It is not too early for children," he said pointedly.

Isabel gathered in Marcelina so that she would not be excluded. "Marcelina will be our child, Lucas."

The small girl's eyes sparkled behind the shawl.

"Yes." His hand caressed Isabel's. "Perhaps when you return for good, there'll be a change. Something growing that wasn't before, perhaps."

"When are you coming to see me?"

"As soon as I can. Next weekend."

"I see," she said, her face opening into a grin. "Will they let me stay with you?"

"We can find a room."

"One with running water inside, perhaps."

"Some have toilets," Marcelina exclaimed, eager to join in.

"And stoves that use gas flames," Isabel added.

Lucas suddenly pointed. "Here is where the canoe came out from the chalets with a passenger." The *Huitzitzil* had gone around the bend from the Santiago laguna, where the chalets rose splendiferously up from the rocky banks. "The house guardian took me back to their property," Lucas continued. "I walked up to the road after that."

Both Marcelina and Isabel peered at the rocks on shore where, weeks before, Lucas had returned from mailing the letter.

Twenty minutes later, they all looked up at the sleeping figure of Tecún Umán, lying in the shape of the mountains and the clefts where the earth reached up for sky, and they tried to make out the bright jewel of Sololá placed like a pendant on the ancient warrior's headdress. Twenty minutes after that, they landed at Panajachel.

Isabel stared wide-eyed at the activity in Panajachel. The area was full of foreigners. Some sat at tables in the open-air restaurants and gazed out across the lake to the volcanoes and hills of the other side. She looked back and saw Oro Hill like a hat at the bottom of

Volcán Tolimán. Dozens of children, some just a little older than Marcelina, flurried in and out of the foreigners with arms draped in bracelets or fists dangling brightly colored stuffed birds or with bundles of clothing perched on their heads. Most of the foreigners paid little attention or waved their arms distractedly as if at pesky insects. Everywhere along the road were makeshift stalls and tables set up to sell clothing, blankets, bags . . . too many things for Isabel, so she focused on Marcelina's shawl swinging at her waist. She concentrated on the silver threads intricately woven into the darker colors to form subtle shapes of spirits.

Isabel walked with the basket atop her head. Lucas walked with Marcelina. They went past the luxuriant Hotel del Lago, where one night cost half a year's salary. They went by quickly, only glancing at the wealthy foreigners entering and leaving through the glass doors. They found themselves thrust into the bustle of Panajachel. They went past the Restaurant El Psicodélico, past the Texas Movie House, past the Café du Lac, past Mein Ziel, and up to the head of the road where the buses came to take them up the mountain to Sololá.

When the bus came, one of the carriers secretly opened the back of the bus to allow them easy entrance. Isabel imagined that he had recently left his village and had recognized their befuddlement in this active town. He closed the door quickly behind them.

All the commotion of foreigners made her not notice the beautiful trip up the mountainside to Sololá. Instead, she tried to invent what she would be had she been born into a life of ease. Perhaps, she thought, she would never have doubts. Perhaps she would not have others imagining her life for her, but she would be the one to decide who she was to become.

The bus traveled twenty minutes to arrive at the east side of the plaza. The carrier boy snapped open the back door. Lucas stepped out and helped him pull down their basket. Then they turned in the direction of the lake. Two blocks later, they turned right and went another block. There, on the southwest corner, was Santa Teresita, a small school stretching one block, with a chapel in the middle, dormitories to the right, and squat buildings to the left. The normal school was in recess: The building was quiet, the entranceway empty. The road was very still. Northward, the street ran straight into the west side of the plaza. Looking southward, and over the bulge of the street, all three felt a sudden relief at seeing the lake spreading in clear view and Oro Hill framed delicately by the two rows of homes on the street. The distance that Lucas and Isabel had envisioned would be between them instantly shrank with that vista. It was likely that she and Marcelina would be able to see Oro Hill from somewhere in Sololá, but she never conceived that it would be so nicely visible from the school. Although Chuuí Chopaló was too small and indistinct to see, it could be imagined there by the lake under the hat-shaped Oro Hill. And that was enough to span the unfortunate distance between her and Lucas.

"Shall we enter?" he said.

Isabel peered through the gate, hoping to see another husband in the compound to make things easier. But there was no one. She nodded and led them through the black iron gate and into the small entranceway. The small arched area opened onto a courtyard with a basketball net. Darkened classrooms were on either side.

"Perhaps I should go," Lucas said.

As soon as he spoke, two women appeared from down the far hallway. One was an albino, and she star-tled them, made them think that these were apparitions coming forward instead of real people.

"Hello," the albino said.

All three of them stared. They had never seen such a thing. They did not know how to react or what to think, did not know what might hurt her feelings or harm them, too.

The albino held her hands together. "My name is Blanca Gloria Tzakol."

Isabel fixed her eyes on Blanca's clothing and knew that she was from San Lucas Tolimán. That made her more real. The other woman was from San Luís Palopó.

The other woman was shy and nervous. "I am Juanita Coytí."

"I'm Isabel Pacay Choy." She introduced Marcelina. She awkwardly introduced Lucas, still unsure of whether he should be inside the school.

The five stood looking at one another for several moments, the basket between them.

Finally, Blanca said, "You will be sharing a room with me."

"Oh," Isabel said.

"There is another woman, too, but she isn't here yet."

"I see," Isabel said.

"And Marcelina, of course." Blanca smiled.

Marcelina stared up at the red eyes and white skin and dared not speak.

"Perhaps I should go," Lucas said awkwardly. "You should unpack, perhaps."

Marcelina clutched at Isabel's hand, and her body edged closer.

Eight

"Good afternoon," Juanita Coytí said, and left Blanca to show Isabel and Marcelina something of the school. Isabel watched the shy young woman's back and thought it would be nice if she didn't feel the need to leave.

"I'll help you," Blanca offered, her hand extended.

Blanca hefted one side of Isabel's basket, and the three went to the end of the courtyard and to the right. She pointed out the empty classrooms with her pursed lips as they passed them. Down the hallway, she gestured with her chin at the open entrance to the small church. They paused just long enough to fill their eyes with the Virgin Mary behind the altar and the proscenium hung with fruits, vegetables, and draping cut paper decorations. Everything else was a warm blur of wood pews and shadowed alcoves barely illumined by the pale light falling from a single stained-glass window behind the altar and barely visible because of the proscenium decorations.

Just the doing of simple things, of walking with the basket between them, of seeing what the new place held, of overcoming Isabel's discomfort with the strange surroundings, helped Blanca become less an exotic sight and more of a real person. Marcelina still cowered on the opposite side of Blanca and looked with astonishment at Blanca's pale flesh, but Marcelina, too, was quickly becoming more interested in the new details of their home than in Blanca. Blanca carried herself with such a strength of presence and a sense of duty to show Isabel and Marcelina their new home that she naturally channeled their attention from her to the surroundings.

On the other side of the church, the short hallway ended at an open patio surrounded by modest dormitories, a double bathroom, showers, and a laundry room. The patio had an apron ceiling, made of thick wood held up by rounded cement columns, which were stripe-webbed by vines. Between the vine-spiraled columns, and evenly spaced in the patio itself, were large clay pots with young jacaranda, ocote, mango, and avocado trees. Everywhere, the vines and plants erupted in fist-sized blooms of white and yellow and red. A mottled turtle moved slowly and ponderously at the foot of this nursery. It immediately snapped Marcelina's attention. She lunged enthusiastically for the broad-shelled creature.

Both Blanca and Isabel chuckled.

"They were brought here long ago by one of the nuns," Blanca said. "That's what a teacher told me." She marveled with the other two, herself still not accustomed to seeing the reptiles. Compared to other regions of Guatemala, the lake area was virtually devoid of turtles and snakes. "I think they're from the east—Zacapa or Chiquimula."

As they stood there, an old green parrot sauntered across the branches of the youthful trees and stood beside them at shoulder level. Its head cocked one way and then another as it first looked at the turtle in Marcelina's hands and then at the three of them. It lifted its flaking gray claw to stroke its beak as if it were a beard. The hard talons clicked softly together under its chin. *"Loq'laj tinimit,"* it said calmly, its pearl of an eye catching light.

Isabel started, then beamed with amusement. Marcelina laughed giddily.

"Loq'laj tinimit," it repeated, its eyes folding shut, then opening in a slow, opalescent wink.

"Ri je'likalaj ub'i' ri nu nan," Isabel said. "The beautiful name of my mother."

The parrot settled its old shoulders and turned partially away. *"Loq'laj tinimit,"* it said, and peered off into sky framed by the open patio.

Blanca grinned. " 'Beloved pueblo' is all it ever says, I think. I haven't heard it say anything else. It keeps repeating it. Last night, it laughed just like one of the girls. Every time she laughed, it did, too."

Marcelina put the turtle down. It lumbered away from her feet. She rose up on tiptoe, head upturned, and gazed at the old parrot.

Blanca spoke to Marcelina's back. "Teacher Xtah calls it Vucub Kaqix, Seven Parrot."

The parrot seemed to prefer being admired than to act as if anything these humans did was of interest. It preened regally, now and then cocking a haughty eye at the featherless ones below.

Isabel scanned the patio more curiously. "What other animals are there?"

Marcelina instantly glanced among the pots and plants, hoping to catch sight of some new wonder.

"I'm not sure," Blanca said.

Before her sister could escape, Isabel said, "There will be time to investigate, Marcelina."

Blanca pointed to the far right corner of the patio area. "Our room is over here."

Isabel gently tugged at Marcelina's *huipil.*

The room had a floor made of dull red tiles, worn to a white buffing in the walking space between the three beds. The walls were stuccoed white and bare except for a heavy wood crucifix and a few long spider webs descending from the high ceiling. A dark brown, nearly black rosary hung from the crucifix; a palm leaf rose behind it. In the center of the room, a single, uncovered light bulb hung from a blackened cord. The light socket was ornate brass, as if, long before the building had been turned into Santa Teresita, it had once formed part of a pretentious chandelier in a ladino home. One wall betrayed the faint outline of a large dresser, now replaced by a simple desk made of three boards. It was too short to use except while sitting on the floor.

Isabel looked back at the beds.

"That one is yours." Blanca indicated the one opposite the door. "They have been assigned."

Isabel put her basket at the foot of the bed and sat. It was a real bed. It had a metal frame with arched headboard and footboard and rods coming down from the arches so that they looked like gates. The mattress itself rested on metal coils and flat boards. It was a single mattress, so soft that Isabel thought it a mistake that she and Marcelina would be allowed to use it. Both Marcelina and Isabel sat down tentatively and tested the fabric and heft of the springs. They squeezed the mattress with their fingers, expecting to hear the crackling of straw. Instead, the cotton-filled mattress yielded softly to them.

"This is wonderful!" Isabel said.

Blanca sat on her bed, in front of Isabel.

She noticed Blanca's carrying case under the bed and scooted her own basket under her frame.

"Did you bring a blanket?"

"Yes."

Blanca rose. "Use this for now," she said, and reached over to the third bed, placed sideways against the short wall under the crucifix. Blanca grabbed the small pillow. "When the other one comes, we will get her a pillow from Maestra Alom."

"Thank you." Isabel looked up at Blanca's face. She studied it, saw the friendliness in the high cheekbones, the pink eyes, the colorless eyebrows. "Thank you," she said again.

Isabel smoothed out the extra pillow in her lap. "You are from San Lucas?"

Blanca settled back on the bed against the wall.

All three sat quietly for a moment. Isabel surveyed everything in the room, as did Marcelina. A mirror hung just visibly behind the tall wood door. From the angle of the bed, Isabel could see that it would cast a warped reflection.

She turned again to Blanca, wanting to get used to her strange appearance. Isabel admired the way Blanca accepted their obvious assessment of her. She handed the pillow to Marcelina. "Do all the rooms have three teachers?" Isabel asked.

72

"I don't know."

Marcelina scrambled her way onto the third bed and jostled the beads hanging from the wall.

"And who is the other one to come?"

Blanca entwined her fingers on her lap. "All I know is that her name is Nina Xbalám. She's from San Pedro la Laguna."

Marcelina stretched out on the third bed.

"Marcelina!"

She hurried back.

Blanca smiled. "She's curious."

"Too curious," said Isabel.

"It's a good thing. Not enough girls are curious. Boys, yes, but girls? We have to do more, to get them to imagine things." She peered at Marcelina. "Do you want to be a teacher?"

Under those glaring pink eyes, Marcelina shriveled.

"It takes a while to get used to me," she said to Marcelina.

Marcelina gripped Isabel's elbow.

"You can look at me all you want. I don't mind."

Marcelina buried one eye into Isabel's side.

"Do you want to know what happened?"

The eye turned out.

"I was born like this." Blanca held out her hands and arms, intorting them so they could see all the flesh of her arms. "I'm an albino. That means that I don't have color in my body." She leaned forward. "People think that I'm a *gringa* at first."

Marcelina smiled uncomfortably.

Isabel was fascinated. Blanca could have looked like a foreigner, yet not really like a foreigner. There was too much comfort in her movements inside the traditional *huipil* and skirt for her to be a foreigner. And her hair was long and straight. Her mouth was thick-lipped and textured, like the White Nun flower. She most definitely did not act like those *gringas* in Panajachel who dressed up in the clothing of the people. Not one of them could ever speak Tzutujil like Blanca.

Blanca held her arms out for inspection. Her skin was pale, barely freckled. Her fingernails were pink, a much lighter pink than her eyes. Marcelina pressed a finger into Blanca's forearm.

"It was a very good thing that I looked like my father the minute I was born." She turned her jaw so they could see her profile clearly. Her hair was even lighter than that of some of the blonde foreigners. Her eyebrows seemed thinner than they actually were, since they revealed the pale flesh beneath. Her eyelashes were like the translucent roots of white corn tassels.

"What do you think?" she said, holding her body at an angle for better viewing.

They marveled.

Blanca settled back decisively, putting an end to her playful self-revealing. "All my life I've been treated badly because of this. Always there are those who want to bother, to torment. In San Lucas, some people wanted my mother to do away with me as soon as I was born. Because of that, I spent most of my time with the Fathers in San Lucas. Once, a man from the United States came and asked me questions about my whole life. I asked him questions, as well. I tell you, it's more important to ask questions than to answer them!" Blanca moved as if to erase the intimacy of her words. "School is the way to learn." She directed her words at Marcelina. "That's the way to learn." She scooted back against the wall.

Isabel felt compelled to speak after such an enigmatic speech. Yet what came out was "Who is Maestra Alom?"

"She's the head teacher. She runs everything."

"Oh."

"She's ladino, I think."

Isabel pushed back on the bed, as well. "How many of us are there?"

Blanca shrugged. "I said I didn't know."

"Oh. Well, how long have you been here?"

"Two days."

Suddenly, Isabel's body felt stiff, uncomfortable, her hands clumsy and blunt. She glanced away and saw a woman standing at the door, watching them.

They all stared at one another, until finally Blanca said, "You are Nina Xbalám?"

"Yes," she said, and crossed to the last bed. She dropped her green vinyl bag.

Isabel observed the woman's back as she gave two quick jabs to feel the mattress. She straightened and stared directly at the crucifix over her bed, at the rosary dangling from it. A small clucking rose from her throat.

"Where are you from?" Isabel asked politely.

She turned. Her attention went around the walls and to the ceiling. Her face was thinner than that of most women of the lake area, with strong cheeks and angry dark eyes. She was taller than normal, over five feet tall, and much taller than Isabel. Her hands remained still at her side, but the fingers seemed tense as if ready to grab or lunge out.

"You are from San Pedro la Laguna," Blanca said, mouthing the polite words between people meeting for the first time; yet she turned them from a question to a statement.

Nina Xbalám barely looked at her. "You are from San Lucas," she said. "You are from Chuuí Chopaló."

"My father is Alfredo Pacay, my mother is Manuela Poc Pacay."

"You're fortunate to have parents."

Blanca and Isabel exchanged glances.

"My mother is dead," Isabel said.

"My father disappeared," Blanca said.

Nina sat on the bed. She glanced first at Blanca, then at Isabel, finally at Marcelina.

To Isabel, Nina's face seemed to be set permanently into a frown. Her dusky eyes were impenetrable, her body too rigid and angry. "We have come, then," Isabel said, as embracively as she could.

"Yes," Nina answered. "We have come."

Nina's gaze did not leave Marcelina.

Before Isabel could introduce Marcelina, Juanita Coytí appeared at the door and told them that there would be a brief meeting in one of the classrooms. They were to come in five minutes.

"Very well," Blanca answered.

"Stay in the patio," Isabel said to Marcelina.

She frowned.

Blanca leaned forward and smiled. "There may be other children. Go and see."

The twelve teacher trainees gathered at the small desks in one of the classrooms along the open courtyard by the entrance. Seated among them were two experienced teachers who did not live in the compound. They looked alike except that one was thin and the other short; both were very attractive with flat, broad foreheads, richly black hair, and thick bodies. The trainees sat with their roommates, waiting for Maestra

76

Alom, their chairs barely large enough to be comfortable. They first took turns giving their names and the
villages they were from. The experienced teachers,
Xtah and Xpuch, led them in this, and then when they
were finished, they all sat staring at the front of the
room like schoolchildren. There was only a plump
envelope of silence, torn by the occasional rasp of a
chair or cleared throat.

Isabel sat with Nina and Blanca in the next-to-last
row of the room. She did not know what was expected
of her, and in such unfamiliar settings it is always better
to keep very still than to draw unwanted attention. She
could see that the teacher trainees were young, not
more than nineteen or twenty years of age. At sixteen,
she was easily the youngest. All were from the "county"
of Sololá, though some came not from the lake villages,
but from hamlets out past the actual town of Sololá en
route to the highway crossroads of Los Encuentros.
Thin Xtah and short Xpuch were somewhat older, in
their late twenties, already carrying themselves with
confidence. Everyone wore traditional clothing, the two
teachers in almost identical skirts and *huipiles*, marking
them as from the town of Sololá. They were Cakchiqueles. Both waited patiently with their hands folded in
their laps, eyes turned forward. On their feet were
brown leather pumps with ankle straps and open sides.

Isabel glanced at her own red plastic sandals, bought
especially for this trip. She peeked at Nina's leather
sandals, so like those the men of Chuuí Chopaló used,
and at Blanca's green plastic ones, so common at village festivals. Most of the other women had bright gell–
plastic sandals, like Isabel's, but some wore a black style
that girls from Chuuí Chopaló wore to church, and
fewer wore expensive leather. At home, Isabel usually

went barefoot, as most of these women probably did, particularly when doing everyday work. It occurred to her, unkindly, that Blanca and Nina probably wore sandals all the time. There was something more experienced and at ease about them, as if they did not have problems with money as her family did. Isabel glanced over at Juanita Coytí, her face inclined forward, her arms crossed beneath her large breasts, the purple birds embroidered on her *huipil* billowing just above her arms. Isabel was certain that Juanita would not wear shoes in her village. Isabel imagined that Juanita, too, was surely wondering what forces in the world had brought her to sit in a classroom with other women who seemed brighter and much more confident. Suddenly, Juanita glanced sidelong and smiled, her mouth bright except for the dark gape of a missing tooth.

Isabel did not like being so quiet in a room full of people she did not know. Yet Nina and Blanca were able to be patient. Perhaps that was another way that they both seemed better prepared than she was. Nina and Blanca were already wiser, already experienced and confident. What would they have to learn about dealing with children and families with uncertain ambitions about learning? How could they devise ways to help the people?

Suddenly, Nina spoke in a whisper from the side of her mouth. "She is your sister, not your daughter."

"Marcelina?" Isabel asked uncertainly.

"That's her name?"

"Yes."

Nina's expression betrayed nothing.

"Why do you ask?"

"Because I want to know," Nina answered.

78

A large motion drew everyone's attention. A white-haired woman in her sixties walked stiffly to the front of the room, her face extraordinarily wrinkled, her thick nose curving under, her eyes graying with age, her skin mottled by the years. When she spoke, it was with the deep, rasping voice of a heavy smoker.

"I am Maestra Alom," she said in Spanish. Her body hunched inside solid black clothing, except for a small, faint pink scarf tied around her throat. Her dress waved around her ankles; the sleeves covered her arms all the way down to chubby wrists. Yet the dress plunged at her neck to reveal cleavage and heavy age spots on her blanching skin. Maestra Alom leaned forward and steadied herself on the desk. Her knuckles were large with arthritis. "I am the director of this program," she said. "I want to welcome you to Sololá and to give you my congratulations for proving yourselves to be among the best in all of Guatemala." Her free hand patted back her closely cut hair. "You should be very proud. There were many who did not make it. But you did. It's because you're not only among the smartest and best prepared, but because you are committed to helping in your villages. Guatemala needs more patriots like you—people who want to make her into something we can be proud of. It is through the education of our children that we may see something different in the future. They are the path and avenue for us all. We think that we lead them, but no—they call to us even without knowing, they reach to us and pull us forward. It is they who invent our future, whether we are aware of it or not! Yet you, as teachers, will act as their guides. Well, it is a mutual thing, this voyage made together: both leading, both following, both taking Guatemala to places farther on."

79

Nina restlessly sucked in air. Isabel tightened the clutch of her fingers.

Maestra Alom's free hand moved to the scarf at her throat. She rubbed a thick finger between scarf and skin, as if she were probing a sensitive area. "But what is Guatemala? Is it in the capital? Is it where the Maya live? Is it in Zacapa? Is it in the United States?"

The trainees muttered.

Maestra Alom moved with difficulty into one of the chairs and sat back, her distended belly pressing against the black cotton of her dress. Her swollen feet were encased in black shoes with short block heels. Her flesh seemed ready to burst from the pressure of the shoes.

"Let me tell you about myself," she said. From out of the great pocket of her cleavage, she withdrew a pack of cigarettes and a small plastic lighter.

The trainees looked about with alarm. Isabel saw that Xpuch and Xtah did not react, and so she quelled the bubble of laughter and shock rising in her chest. She waited to see what else Maestra Alom would do, this uncommon woman who smoked and dressed in black and spoke so oddly.

Maestra Alom placed a cigarette into her mouth and flicked it lit. She heaved out an enormous cloud and immediately coughed several times. She gained composure and continued, cigarette held firmly at the side of her mouth.

"My father was Cakchiquel, my mother Tzutujil. They left the lake before I was born to go to the capital to work as servants in ladino homes. It was the best way to live at the time. This is much before your time, my daughters. Much earlier. At the beginning of this century, at the start." Her eyes slitted down to barely open as the blue smoke curled about her face. "In those days, my parents did not do so well with their mixed marriage. Who knows what they thought about? Who knows what the history of our two families created? We know, do we not, that the Cakchiqueles and the Tzutujiles were enemies long before the Castellano came. My grandparents, my forefathers, were not happy with my parents' marriage. They did not appreciate this union. So my father and mother went to the capital to find jobs as servants for the ladino people. Well, this is what they did for many years, forgetting their languages, forgetting their customs and their clothing, as they went on with their work in the capital. Among the ladino and Castellano, they forgot who they were. They taught me to forget who I was, as well. *Pues*, I was only a servant. A child of servants. Only that. Do you see?"

Many of the trainees feebly assured her that they did.

"I became a young girl in the city. Every Sunday we went out walking the parks and boulevards where the people sold *chuchitos*, tamales, and *atole de maíz*. There we were all servants, *la muchedumbre*, as they called us. When I was older, they built the zoo and the statue of Tecún Umán. We started to go there. Have you been there?"

Only no's answered her.

She smiled up to the ceiling and sucked her cigarette. Her fingers fumbled a moment and pulled the long-ashed cigarette from her mouth. She still gazed at the ceiling and did not notice the ash fall to her lap. When she looked down again, her eyes opened wide as if she had forgotten where she was, what she was speaking about. And then, just as suddenly, the clarity returned to her expression.

"I tell you, my first twenty-five years I ignored what

81

I was. I ignored my people. The next twenty-five years, I spent all my time, all my energy, trying to find my life in the faces living among the towns and hamlets, here in the cocksfoot among the volcanoes. My last twenty-five years will be spent learning to accept what I am. I have lost and won, I have forgotten and remembered. What remains as true is that I am the one to sit with myself for the rest of my days. That is my task, my office: to know what the world has made of me. I give this to you," she said in Tzutujil. She repeated it in Cakchiquel and again in Quiché. She leaned back in the seat and concentrated on her cigarette. The smoke billowed out from her upturned face. "To see what the world has made of me," she said to the ceiling.

They watched Maestra Alom smoke. She seemed not to notice them, however, and after a prolonged moment, the teachers rose from their seats and walked outside to the courtyard. Xtah waited by the door until the trainees followed, Isabel among the last, she was so enthralled by Maestra Alom. The old woman seemed not to notice their leaving either. She was lost in the swirls of her cigarette smoke, mirroring the labyrinths of private thought in the space between her head and the ceiling.

Outside, Xpuch explained, in a voice startlingly deep for someone so short, that they had the rest of the day free, that dinner would be served in the cafeteria, and did everyone know where that was?

Too few knew.

Xtah and Xpuch began to explain at the same time, stopped, and started again. They sputtered. Xtah began alone. She explained that there was a corridor in front of the chapel, and didn't everyone see it as they had come in? Most had, but had ignored its importance. Then came the nursing station, the sick beds, the kitchen and cafeteria. And there was the open field where the children played soccer during the school year. It was walled off so that no one could enter, with a gate blocking the field from the hallways so that no one had to fear intruders at night. Down there, in plain sight, was the cafeteria. It was easy to see. So, continued Xpuch, they could walk in the town as they pleased until dinner at seven, and the school would begin for them at eight in the morning.

The young women stood awkwardly about as they paired up or grouped by room and decided what they would do. The teachers stood to the side and waited to see if anyone had questions. Isabel glanced at Blanca and Nina. Blanca grinned. Nina looked away and toward the door of the school.

Isabel wanted to walk for a bit with Marcelina and perhaps Blanca. She felt guilty for already disliking Nina without really knowing her. It was just the abrasive way she had of staring and ignoring others and of speaking so curtly.

"Shall we go?" Blanca asked Isabel.

"Yes."

Nina did not answer.

"I'll get Marcelina," Isabel said.

She left them standing a few feet apart, silent, Blanca's hands hidden in her shawl, Nina's hands clasped behind her back. When she returned with Marcelina in tow, both women smiled.

"Ready?" Blanca asked.

All four walked out the door, Blanca and Nina in front and Isabel and Marcelina behind. They stopped in the street, looked one way, then the other, judging with new eyes their place in the town now that they had been welcomed in and made a part of Sololá.

Directly in front of Santa Teresita was a small park and field where children played. A streetlight opposite the entrance to the school had graffiti depicting the fist and rose of the Democratic Socialist Party. The road sloped down sharply to the right, concealing the road just beyond the next corner, where a pastel blue-and-green store advertised Rubio cigarettes. Men worked to cut a trench across the street alongside the store. The lake appeared like a hazy blue over their shoulders, and past that, on the far shore, Oro Hill faintly bulged at the feet of the magisterial Volcán Tolimán.

To their left, the gray stone road ascended to the center of town. On the near corner, a pastel blue-and-green pharmacy advertised Panadol. Several trainees gathered there. Far up the hill, the old church with its pink-and-white tower was just visible above the lower buildings on the hill. To the immediate left, on the external wall joining the school chapel and dormitory building, someone had written *URNG* in red letters— the sign for the union of national revolutionary parties of Guatemala.

"This is not seen in Chuuí Chopaló," Blanca said, pointing at the letters. Nina walked on disinterestedly.

Isabel was glad that Blanca had pointed out the emblem. It was true: There were no political markings on the south side of the lake, or at least never any of the guerrilla or revolutionary parties. Only the established Christian Democrats or the various conservative and paramilitary parties. Yet, ironically, the south side had the reputation for insurgency, not the north side.

More trainees appeared from the doorway of the

pharmacy. They drank sodas through bright plastic straws.

"Shall we get something to drink?" Isabel asked.

Nina shrugged. "It's too crowded. Perhaps on the way back."

Thankfully, for Isabel, when they turned left at the corner, they saw three trainees walking down that road. Two small children walked with them. It felt odd not to join up with them, not to be a part of their activities in order to get to know them. At least they were walking the same route.

They continued past the barred entranceway of their health center. They stopped to peer through the gate at the open field past the hallway. On the next corner, they stopped and looked up and down the cross street. Northward and up, toward the center of town, there were several stores and an odd clutch of wood shacks with a sign declaring the place a video saloon.

"Movies!" Blanca exclaimed.

"Surely, American movies," Nina grumbled.

Isabel and Marcelina exchanged private wide-eyed expressions of excitement. "We've never been to one," Isabel said.

Both Blanca and Nina turned in surprise.

"You are better for it," Nina stated flatly.

Down the crossroad there were homes, and on the corner a large modern building for the School of Communication and Science. They continued past that, where the stone road became dirt, and they came upon a huge soccer field. A makeshift game was in progress. Against the far wall, a group of girls watched the boys play. Those girls sat together, touching, faces pressing close together, one woman combing the hair of another, not like the four of them, who walked as if they did not have the same language, as if they did not share the same world or experiences. Isabel held Marcelina's hand more tightly.

Beyond the soccer field, the road sloped up another hill to overlook the whole lake. At the top of the road was an abandoned school in a very modern building. The windows were broken, the grass overgrown with weeds, and the wall and fence broken or knocked down in various places. The very front of the school had large wood doors badly chipped with bullet holes. An X of wood slats was nailed from one side of the door frame to the other. At the bottom of the sealed door, an emaciated female dog lay curled. She barely raised her head at the four trespassers. Her swollen teats lay bulging against the cracked and cool cement stoop. Her pups were nowhere to be seen.

The four of them leaned against the guardrail in front of the school to gaze out over the lake. To their right, on the far side, Volcán Atitlán now could be seen like a taller twin standing just behind Tolimán. The Santiago lagoon curved at the feet of these titans and kept the town of Santiago Atitlán hidden from sight. Volcán San Pedro rose straight up from the west shore, with half of the village of San Pedro la Laguna visible beneath the vast ledge two hundred meters below where they stood. On this near land, there were compounds with thatch and cornstalk huts or stone huts with corrugated metal roofs. The open land between compounds bristled with corn and beans. This same plateau extended below them to the left and concealed the rest of the south shore after Oro Hill and Chuuí Chopaló. San Lucas Tolimán was hidden. Farther to the left, the soccer field, lower lands, and cemetery of Sololá completely obscured the west shore of the lake with its towns of Santa Catarina, San Luís Palopó, and Godínez.

The vista was panoramic, expansive, and chilling in its beauty. The air was light and cool; the peaks of the volcanoes and the burrs of the mountains snagged and shredded the eastward-moving clouds so that the clouds were left spindling across the vault of sky at such an altitude that only the loom of heaven could weave them back together. Down below, in the bottom of the sphere made by the arc of sky and the bowl of lake, the boat from Santiago made its tiny way northward back to Panajachel. It looked like a thin white brushstroke, an old woman's eyelash, in that blue canvas of lake.

"This is beautiful," Isabel said.

Not one would dare say otherwise.

"I don't know if I'm ready for this," Isabel said.

Nina looked at her and spoke in a gentle, earnest voice, not in one that tried to fight or argue. "What makes you think this is real?"

Blanca cocked her head. "Eh?" she said.

Marcelina pulled away to slide her hand along the top edge of the guardrail.

Nina turned her back to the vista. "The government never really does things to help people. They make promises, but promises are nothing but breaths of air. This is probably another plan to get money from the United States. They don't care about us. That's why they have us here, with a crazy woman for a director and One Monkey and One Howler for teachers."

Marcelina stared in shock at Nina's ridicule of the teachers.

"Why are you so angry?" Blanca asked.

Nina smirked. "Why *aren't* you angry?"

They locked eyes.

87

"Even if the training lasts the full period," Nina continued, "the program will run out of money before we get the jobs, and we will be in the same place as before. Teachers will suffer as before."

"Some of us will be wiser," Blanca added.

"And what does that do?"

"I have my plans."

"Oh, well!" Nina said, with no attempt to hide her sarcasm.

Blanca simply pushed off the railing and started back down the hill. Isabel gave a questioning glance to Nina, but the other woman stood by dispassionately.

"You're an angry woman," Isabel said.

Nina lifted her arms to take in the whole vista. "For my country," she said affectedly. "And what do you get angry about?"

Isabel ignored her. She indicated Blanca, already nearing the end of the abandoned school area. "And her? Why do you have to make her angry? What does that do?"

Nina sat back against the railing. Her red-and-blue skirt tightened around her thighs. "She does not need my opinion of her."

Isabel waved for Marcelina. "Come on," she said, and took hold of her sister's small hand. She felt suddenly shy and stupid because of the argument. She didn't even understand what the problem was, just that Nina was full of tension and Blanca had tried to be nice.

"Good afternoon," Isabel said, and wished that she didn't feel the need to leave.

Likin

Nine

The first week, Isabel felt as if she were spinning free of the earth, there was so much activity and excitement and newness. Her mind reeled with the unfamiliar and the insights into the other young teachers, who were like her in some ways, yet quite different in others.

Every morning, Isabel arose with Marcelina and the trainees just after dawn, the dusky and mist-filled air casting its own shadowed presence within the lighted dormitory. The parrot, Vucub Kaqix, prattled among the nursery trees, particularly if any birds descended from the outside world to investigate his private and woody domain. The turtles plodded out below the plants to capture the spray of sun through the chilled air. The young women walked bleary-eyed into the patio, mostly untalkative, and waited their turn for the two facilities. In that space, faint and alluring threads of woodsmoke eventually pulled them drowsily toward the dining room. There, they ate eggs and tortillas and drank extra-sweet coffee. As they ate, dreamy voices perked up and their minds unfurled from the womb of sleep.

Isabel learned by the third morning that Blanca was better left alone until after her third cup of coffee. Nina seemed always alert, ever ready to comment on what had been discussed the day before in classes or what had fluttered its way into their ears from *El Diario* or *La Prensa Libre,* the two newspapers readily available to them in Sololá. Mostly, Nina criticized everything. Marcelina hung close to Isabel as her older sister listened to Nina point out the deceit of this bit of news or that piece of information. Blanca looked on with incredulity. Isabel simply questioned. Marcelina, a quaking urn, spilled over from the bewildering flood of concepts and debates and perched more closely by Isabel.

After breakfast, the trainees swept the hallways, dining room, and dormitories and cleaned the toilet and shower facilities. By eight o'clock, they were seated in the morning class with Xtah, who explained to them how to teach rather than what to teach. Isabel had expected to learn new ideas of the world and how to adapt them to the old ways of thinking, but the morning lessons focused on how to plan schedules, how to arrange furniture for optimum learning and discussion, how to teach various levels of students at the same time, how to make children follow in single file from the classroom to the playground, and more important things, like how to adapt to economic failings in a village when it was impossible to obtain books, chalkboard, desks or chairs, or even walls and a roof. They talked about how to take advantage of the stuff of everyday life for lessons in history, math, and oral literature. They discussed what could be done with families and communities that had no funds for food during the midday break. And how to encourage a family that felt work in the field was more important than school. The trainees were challenged to draw upon their own experiences growing up in small hamlets and to envision what would have made their experiences better, more fruitful, something illuminating. Always, the discussion wound its way back to lack of money, lack of full community support, lack of the ability to stand high enough to look out of the abyss of subsistence living, the privileging of males. And then Xtah took that line of frustrating discussion and knotted its end into a statement of the wonderful possibilities for the future.

Nina began these discussions animatedly, speaking more and more emotionally about the poverty and problems with governmental support, how everyone was a servant to everyone else, how people needed to work together to overcome these problems. As the general discussion went inexorably away from the darkness of reality and toward the brightness of Xtah's imagined future, Nina settled into an arm-crossed slump and made grunting, throaty sounds. Blanca, on the other hand, traveled the other direction. She spoke little at first, rolled her eyes at the vision of impotence growing monstrous before her, and only joined in toward the end when Xtah began conjuring the calendars of the future, where the days would be numbered by the successes of these trainees sitting before her. Blanca crossed and uncrossed her legs with great excitement at this. She never failed to mention that she was someone who had risen above the difficulties of reality, that she was one who could go past the limits put upon her by the will of forces greater than hers. And this, for her, was the greatest proof of what the future could be for all of them. Somehow, everything Xtah discussed managed to find its way to relating to Blanca's life and her experience as a mistreated, ill-lucked person who persevered and vanquished all misfortune.

By late morning, Blanca was too excited to remain silent, yet Nina was cast into a sullen quiet. Isabel moved her head from side to side, watching Nina and Blanca as if she were caught up in a fast-paced soccer game. Two other women, Luci Pac and Angela Sicajá, spoke out as well, but not nearly as intrusively as Blanca and Nina. Those two spoke so strongly, particularly when Nina was still vocal and when Blanca was just blossoming, that each of the trainees soon found her particular station in the discussions and debates.

Every hour, they took a ten-minute break. It seemed that the other trainees grouped well together during these times. They sat along the edge of the basketball court or against the doorway to see what they could on the streets. But Nina, Blanca, and Isabel found their office in being the problematic group. The other women kept a safe distance, not without some humor, yet always conscious of being polite. Mostly, the others stayed away from the dynamic Nina and Blanca and let the electricity between them crackle as it would, light up when it did, spark and snap how it might. Occasionally, Angela or Luci entered the fray with a well-placed sentence. And every so often, Juanita or María Tun or one of the other women looked at Isabel with sympathetic eyes, glances that conveyed to Isabel a fear that she would find herself ignited between the high polarities of the other two.

Blanca, Isabel soon realized, was ferociously intelligent. She spoke with a precision and correctness of language that made Isabel feel embarrassed and self-conscious. In her heart, Blanca believed that anyone could rise up to accomplish anything, that it was drive and desire that made all the difference in the world. Nina spoke in plain language, but with an intensity and anger about poverty that made Isabel feel uncomfortable. When Nina spoke, Isabel had the sometimes uncontrollable urge to look over her shoulder and see who might be overhearing the conversation. Maestra Alom would sit in the classroom or outside during the breaks and smoke her cigarettes with one eye closed and the other glazed over, yet staring in their direction. Maestra Alom rarely spoke that first week. Isabel began to feel that it had been a mistake that she was given the honor of being included in the training program. She was quickly convincing herself that it was all a confusion created by an overly confident Andrés Xiloj.

At eleven, the students went back to their rooms to do chores, write letters, wash clothes at the *pila*, reflect, and study what they needed to study. Here, too, when not involved with chores, Isabel's two roommates were very different. Nina wrote frantically to family and friends—some in the capital, Isabel learned to her amazement. Nina would rarely look up as she wrote. When she did glance up, her eyes were lost to the distance. She wrote too slowly for her own taste, as was clear by the way she would scribble hurriedly, stop in a small explosion of irritation, and wiggle her hand as if to jostle free a cramp of slowness bogging down her messages.

Blanca read voraciously. Isabel discovered that Blanca had only two complete changes of clothing. The rest of her pack was filled with paperback books. Some were on the history of Latin America, others on mathematics and biology. When she entered the world of the

94

pages, the book itself seemed to grow into a shield that hid Blanca's pale and studious face. It seemed an act of supplication the way she turned her face down into the book, the way her fingers picked free the next thin vellum, the way the sighs rose out of her as if from her spirit.

Isabel watched these two with fascination. Isabel had neither people to write to—only Andrés Xiloj called to her in that way, since no one else she knew could read well—nor books to read. Unfortunately, she had no idea where Xiloj was. She longed to send him a letter to ask if what she was experiencing was within the bounds of normalcy. Perhaps she would try to understand her feelings about her mother's death in a private letter to him. She, of course, had never had enough money to own books. When she did have books in the past, it was because she had borrowed them from Xiloj. Even then, she had to be secretive because of her mother's displeasure. Now, she neither wrote nor read. Instead, Isabel watched her roommates for a time, and then she and Marcelina would sit on the lip of the patio walkway and talk together about the classes or about the things Marcelina had discovered in the small garden. Often, Isabel sat with Angela, who had her son, and María Tun, whose daughter came in the afternoons. That first week, Marcelina and the other two children discovered two turtles, four snakes, and three blue green lizards. Always, Vucub Kaqix sauntered over to peer down at them. He pretended to be too important to hear the trivial things these humans talked about, while hoping all along that they would appreciate how beautiful he was, how like the sun he was. The children invariably gave in.

That first week, too, Isabel discovered that neither

Angela nor María had a mother left alive, and María had a brother who was disappeared. Not one of them cried. The children sat tightly beside the older women and looked wide-eyed at one another.

Just before one o'clock, all of them made their way to the dining room for lunch. There, the conversation turned to what people would be doing after siesta or what they did the day before. Since no one talked about the classes, both Nina and Blanca grew silent. They seemed two entirely different people from when they were dominating all discussion during class or between class breaks. This was the time when the other trainees mentioned their lives, their homes, their husbands, if they had any. Blanca watched with a bored expression and ate dutifully through her meal, a hearty soup of chicken or squash or tripe. Nina ate more slowly because, though silent, she was intent on what the other women said about their lives. She never asked questions or spoke, but listened to the women talk about their problems with husbands, their desires to be something other than what they were expected to be. Isabel told how she had almost lost Lucas because she wanted to become a teacher and how her mother had been gravely ill. María and Angela nodded kindly. She told them about Alan Waters, the American who had studied medicine in Chuuí Chopaló, and she told, with hardly an embellishment, about her marriage to Lucas. Nina listened with such interest and Blanca with such disinterest that Isabel did not know what to think of these two women, who erupted and quieted with such irregular quickness.

After eating, they cleaned up the dining room. Many of the trainees returned to their rooms to sleep for an hour, then have free time before the three o'clock classes. More often than not, in that first week, Isabel spent this free time of day with Marcelina. Once, she took the other children on a walk so the mothers could converse alone.

At three, the students entered the classroom with Xpuch to discuss different issues, mostly about Guatemalan history and major writers of the twentieth century. All of it was ladino culture, and nothing about the heritage of the people. When the people were discussed, it was always through the mouths and perceptions of the ladino or the Spanish. Because of this, the sessions were reversed from the morning for Blanca and Nina. Blanca began excitedly because of the focus on history and ideas, and Nina began with an irritated hush at the lack of social context. Blanca showed off so much, it seemed to Isabel, and with such knowledge, that after three days, Xpuch rarely made a statement without glancing at Blanca to make sure she had not erred. But by the end of the afternoon sessions, it was Blanca who sat smoldering and Nina who argued enthusiastically with Xpuch.

On Wednesday, in exasperation, Blanca capped the afternoon by saying, "Why does everything have to be political?"

Nina leaned forward to look past Isabel and at Blanca. "Everything is political whether we want it to be or not."

"This is what you say," Blanca answered.

"What seems to be not political is only what is the accepted ways. Because it is so accepted, we just think it is truth."

Maestra Alom sighed a blue cloud of smoke so loudly that all of them turned in their seats to look. She cleared her throat and smiled at Isabel. "Something hidden only seems to be gone," she said enigmatically, then returned to her strange, popeyed observation of the class.

At six, the classes finished for the day and the students had some time before nightfall to relax with another walk or to read and write letters. A light supper at eight-thirty ended the day, and the students returned to their rooms and were asleep by nine-thirty or ten. Marcelina slept beside Isabel, her face turned to the small space between bed and wall, the cover pulled comfortingly up to her mouth. The three women lay still in the dark and let their minds find their own separate points of rest. On Thursday, Isabel turned on her side and spoke across the space between the beds.

"You are both very smart," she said.

Though no answer came back across the darkness—what could either of them say? An answer was not expected—Isabel felt them take in her words, purl them with thought. She could sense their appreciation in the subtle changes in their breathing and in the gravity of their presence. Yet neither spoke.

On Friday, Lucas appeared at the school gate. He waited patiently until recess, and then he observed Isabel speaking with Nina and Blanca for several moments before calling out. He entered at Isabel's request. The other women were excited to meet him, though he was too shy to do anything but nod when names were exchanged. Isabel walked him back to the gate.

He leaned into her once they were out of sight. His arms gathered her in, and his mouth brushed close to her ear. "I want you to come back," he whispered. "I miss you."

From where they stood, Isabel could see Chuuí

Chopaló at the foot of Tolimán. It seemed like a sprout of the parent volcano.

"Come back for the weekend," he said. His face pressed alongside hers.

She drew back from the pleasurable touch of his skin. "I can't. I'm sorry, but there's a visit by the program officials tomorrow. It's our opportunity to show that their plan has been put to good use."

His eyes darkened with disappointment. He seemed ready to say something, but he did not.

She squeezed his hand in hers. "Can you take Marcelina while I finish today?"

He nodded. He pulled her against him once more, kissed her mouth, then released her. In minutes, Marcelina came skipping out and took hold of his hand. He affectionately rubbed the top of her head. Isabel urged Marcelina to take him where she and Isabel walked: up to the abandoned school, past the soccer field, to get a wide view.

"I'll meet you up there," she said, her mind trying to stop its airy reeling from the almost physical thoughts of Lucas and from her longing for his familiarity.

Ten

Lucas had rented a room away from the center. It was in a slat wood building higher up on the slopes on a stretch of street leading out of town, not far from the main avenue, yet far enough away to be cheap. One fence of the compound was destroyed, and the yard inside held splintered barrels, pieces of scavenged equipment, a listing porcelain toilet, and many sore-tormented chickens. Everything—the wicker chairs outside the room, the stuccoed walls, the air itself—smelled of fire, though there was no fire to be seen.

The door to his room barely closed, and that only with a loop of string hanging from a nail in the frame. Daylight shone through the slats inside the room and revealed the narrow street just outside. It was a back road. There were heaps of broken stone and dried brush directly across from him. He could just make out a dog scavenging in the debris-spattered ravine on the far side, its gray body blending in with the trash and dry clay. Near Lucas, just on the other side of his wall, paper clung to a coil of barbed wire. He could have stuck a finger between the slats and bloodied it, if he'd been careless. Inside, there was only a small end table with an oil lamp, and the bed, a straw-stuffed mattress atop six boards within a wood frame. The owner of the room, a woman with a huge burn scar across one side of her face, asked him for five quetzales. "In Santiago they charge only two quetzales," he complained. She said that he was welcome to stay in Santiago if it was more convenient for him. It was for one night only, he pleaded. She sniffed and lowered it to four quetzales, her palm held out.

They would not be able to spend much money. He had enough for the boat and bus to Chuuí Chopaló, but only pennies left over for food. He carefully folded the remaining bills around his coins and tucked the small cache into his waist sash. Marcelina took hold of his hand, and they walked through some narrow and empty streets to the main avenues leading into the center. Marcelina led him down by the movie huts, where they paused to look at what was left of ripped movie posters. One depicted large-breasted foreign women in cages, their clothing torn and revealing, a group of dark-skinned men threatening them with whips. Another poster had been stripped away, and only the bare feet of a woman and her disembodied head remained. She had blue eyes and blonde hair, and the sun was setting just beyond her. The writing was all in English.

Lucas and Marcelina continued to the soccer field, where they watched some young men playing. Lucas did not speak much. His hands warmheartedly brushed Marcelina's hair, formed over her skull, tugged her nearer to him, but his mind was on Isabel and the inconvenience of their separation. He lifted Marcelina up to the stone wall so they could better see the players, and he leaned forward to rest his crossed arms beside her. The men dribbled and passed. It was not a real game. They stopped frequently to show off. No one seemed to mind. Some very young boys and girls aped the game far on the other side.

"Has it been fun, Marcita?"

Marcelina shrugged, not really sure what Lucas was referring to.

"You don't get bored sitting in the room all day?"

"A little bored," she answered. "I play with Tomás and Sinta, and with the animals in the patio. There're turtles and snakes and a parrot. It says 'My beloved pueblo.' Isabel always answers with 'That is the beautiful name of my mother.'"

Lucas chuckled appreciatively. "And the others?"

Marcelina shrugged again.

"You don't like them very much."

"They argue all the time. I don't know what they're talking about."

Lucas picked up tiny pebbles on the wall and bounced them on the space before him.

"They talk about school," he directed.

"Yes."

"And about their husbands."

"They aren't married."

"There are no men who come to talk with them?"

"No."

"But they speak about men."

Marcelina shifted uncomfortably on the wall. "No."

Lucas looked out at the players. One knocked the

ball into the air with his forehead, counting the successive times.

"Well, the albino is very strange."

"Yes," Marcelina said enthusiastically. "Blanca is very smart. And very nice."

"Nicer than the other one?"

"Yes! Nina is always angry. She speaks rudely." Marcelina shifted around on the wall. "And she interrupts all the time."

Lucas scattered his handful of pebbles. "Are you ready?"

Marcelina nodded and waggled her hips out for Lucas to lift her. He floated her down beside him. They walked up the hill to the abandoned school overlooking the lake. Marcelina skittered ahead. Lucas ambled calmly, looking out and around to take in the whole area. Up by the barred door, three military men sat eating lunch. One of the men opened up a fat loaf of bread with a knife the length of his forearm. The other two smiled and nodded at Lucas. *"Buenos,"* they called. Lucas said hello back and joined Marcelina by the railing. A few feet below them, a solitary puppy scratched and sniffed at a hole at the base of a stone ledge.

"There's Oro Hill," Marcelina said. Her finger poked through the air.

Lucas took in the full view: the blue green platter of the lake, the volcanoes rising darkly up into the clear sky, the curving green lands below with their smudges of gray and brown where the villages were, and the different views of the hamlets of Sololá: the white hotel on the promontory to the far left; the plateau below with the compound; the stepped lands to the right. He sat beside Marcelina and enjoyed the warm sun on his face

103

and arms. His eyelids dropped. He did not speak. His hands rested softly on his thighs, the fingers curling, his back arching down.

When at last they felt that too much time had passed, Lucas and Marcelina left the panorama and walked back alongside the soccer field. They waited in the small park in front of Santa Teresita. After many minutes, Marcelina crossed the avenue and entered the gate. She did not reappear for half an hour.

"Isabel is getting lunch," Marcelina explained when she returned.

Lucas touched the money at his waist.

Several more minutes passed before Isabel walked out with her shawl tied in a sling across her front. She stepped quickly, her long, braided hair lashing up at one side and then the other with its black tip. She had brought them tortillas and some cheese and chiles. Lucas counted out some money and sent Marcelina to the corner to buy one soda.

"Let's sit here," Isabel said. A small, grassy spot by a flat rock allowed a clear view of the lake and Oro Hill.

Lucas sat on the rock. Isabel sat sideways on the grass. She spread out her shawl like a tablecloth beside him and arranged the tortillas tied in a rag, the banana leaf with cheese, the small handful of chiles, and a pinch of salt in a tiny wrap of plastic. Isabel carefully unfolded the banana leaf and drained the water from around the goat cheese.

"Is this all right?"

"Wonderful," he said. He reached out and ran the tip of his finger along her collarbone.

Marcelina came back with a plastic bag of Naranjita and a blue straw.

"Here we are," Lucas said.

He pulled pieces of cheese free with his fingers and daubed them onto a tortilla. He rolled it, took a bite, chewed for a moment, then bit a nose-sized chile in half. Isabel crumbed a bit of the moist cheese onto a tortilla for Marcelina and sprinkled salt over it. Both Isabel and Marcelina ate small amounts of the cheese and ate their rolled tortillas much more slowly than did Lucas, making sure that he would have what he wanted before they took too much. The sun was warm over their shoulders. Lucas sat above them; Isabel and Marcelina curled their legs under and leaned elbows onto the rock. Two blue birds waddled near them, their eyes trained on the food yet wary of quick movements. The air smelled faintly of cooking fires, and the faint voices of children sprinkled into their small picnic.

They had nearly finished when Isabel said, "I will have to go clean this afternoon. Classes will be canceled. We have to prepare."

"For the inspection?" Lucas asked.

"They're coming tomorrow. We'll have lunch with them, I think. Maybe tomorrow we'll have the classes for today."

"Then I won't stay late tomorrow."

"It won't take long, the cleaning."

Lucas looked off into the distance.

"Afterward, we can walk." Isabel turned to Marcelina. "Tonight you'll be able to sleep here with Blanca and Nina."

Marcelina's eyes widened so suddenly that Isabel snorted with a suppressed laugh. "Don't worry. There's nothing to worry about."

"With Nina?" she asked.

Isabel chuckled. "With Blanca. I'll be with Lucas. At his room."

"I saw it," Marcelina said. And then as an after-thought, she said, "It cost four quetzales."

"She asked for five," Lucas added. His cheek bulged with food.

Isabel smiled. "Yet you got her to take four!"

Marcelina passed Lucas the last of the orange soda, but he declined.

"Drink it," he told her. His fingers fluttered in a gracious wave.

Isabel tossed the banana leaf into the grass and wrapped the rest of the things into her shawl, including the soda bag and straw.

"Throw it," Lucas said.

"Inside," Isabel answered. "Nina says we need to learn not to throw things away. She says we're getting as bad as Americans, we waste so much."

Lucas smirked.

"Even you have said as much," she replied.

He pulled her up by the hand. "Come on."

They walked down the street, in the direction of the lake, Marcelina in the middle, yanking at their hands, wanting to be lifted and dangled, or else pulling forward or tugging them into a full stop. They strolled slowly, looking into open doorways, into open gates, saying hello to people sitting before homes or by storefronts. Isabel could not have felt more married than she did.

"You don't ask," said Isabel, finally, "but I want to tell you."

He hip-hopped Marcelina in the air. "Tell me, then."

"I love it! Every day there's so much to learn." She felt her heart beating and told herself that they had plenty of time, no need to rush.

The way went straight for several blocks, then curved behind a huge and leafy pine tree. The cross street thinned to a dirt path, concealed by overhanging branches and broken limbs. Lucas led them along the clear way.

"Blanca can answer all the questions the teachers ask. She knows everything, it seems. When we're talking about math or science, Blanca is always the one who answers. Even when it's not a question, Blanca will speak out about this thing or that thing, which suddenly gives us all more knowledge than we had before. She'll raise her hand and say, 'I wonder, did you know that Jupiter has rings like Saturn?'" Isabel laughed at the uncommonness of it. "She's very odd."

"Where did she learn so much?"

"When she was young, a man and a woman from the United States came into San Lucas as missionaries. She said that they stopped her in the street when she was out walking with her aunt. They went with Blanca and her aunt to her house. In no time, they had spoken many times with the family. After that, they brought her books, paper, and pencils, things she used at school. She said that she had a very good teacher at school, too, but that these foreigners taught her more than anyone else. They were very generous, Lucas. Long after they returned to the United States, Blanca still received books and magazines and letters. Perhaps it was that she was so white, like them. Perhaps they thought she wanted them to help her, or perhaps her family received money from them. Anyway, that's how she learned so much. It was from those foreigners who came into San Lucas to work with the church. Those Americans.

"Blanca said that she wants more than anything to go to school in the United States. She said that there a person can really learn about the world."

Lucas frowned. "Sounds like you."

"Well, I don't see how she would be able to live away from her family. I couldn't, but she said that she'd be able to do it without difficulty. Imagine that. How would she be able to afford living in that place? I don't know. She said she would do anything so long as she could go there to study. What do you think of that?"

He only shook his head.

"Nina, on the other hand, says that she would never go to the United States even if they paid her thousands of quetzales. That one"—Isabel sighed—"is angry with everyone. When we have our classes, she speaks without raising her hand. She just moves her head and speaks out. She'll say, 'And why don't you mention all those who have died because of the military? Why don't you say what we all know is true? That every day our people are disappearing, that they are found dead in the streets, that our people have no food or water or land to raise even a little bit for their families? Why do you pretend that none of that exists? Why do we have this blindness?' She is a very odd one."

"Hmm," he said. "And dangerous!"

"Yesterday, after Marcelina and I went to bed, those two argued for so long that I thought we would never be able to sleep. Nina said that the school is a deception. She said that we're stupid to trust what we've been given. She said that we mean nothing to the government and that this school is surely an invention by people with power who want to imagine us the way they wish. Yet we are the ones who must imagine our own lives! We have to wake up! Blanca didn't say anything to that. According to Nina, the program will not last the two months. It'll end just like the abandoned school on the hill."

Lucas perked up. "Could it really happen?"

"I don't know."

"This is important, Isabel." He paced in front of her. "Maybe you should leave now. If it happens, we've wasted all our time. We will have made a mistake. Who knows if they'll send the money?"

"They already paid a quarter of it."

"But that might be all!"

Isabel guffawed. "They'll pay."

"You have to find out."

"I will," she answered, and took Marcelina's hand.

They moved down the street.

"What does Blanca say about this?"

"She thinks Nina can never see anything but death."

Lucas slapped his thighs. "These two don't seem to be very good roommates for you, particularly with Marcita."

"I just don't know, Lucas. I like to listen to them. I want to listen to them all night and all day. I don't know why, but I do. Sometimes when they finish they're so angry that they just stop, but my mind goes on and on, so I can hardly sleep. I want them to be friendly just so I can hear them again. Is that selfish? Sometimes when I wake up, it feels like I was the one fighting, that I was wrestling with someone in my dreams."

They went through the curve of road and found themselves by the cemetery entrance, a squat building

109

painted aquamarine. Next to that, a black iron gate led into the lawn. Music and prayers made their way out to them from the building.

Lucas gladly changed the subject. "Shall we see?"

They peered curiously through the open doorway at the ceremony inside. Isabel quickly crossed herself and said a prayer for her mother. It was a small gathering of mostly ladinos. Past the building, through the gate, the hallway became tiled with ochre and beige. On one pastel blue wall a polished stone commemorated the Sololá Lions' Club for the money donated to build the chapel and iron gate.

They moved onto the cemetery lawn and the gravel paths between mausoleums. The first row of units were all large and ornate, some with fenced plots, some with statues, some with large carved crests, some with highly polished stone facades. These were the wealthy families of Sololá. Isabel read the names aloud: Rodas, Marroquín, Girón, Cabrera. None of these names reappeared on the plain pastel foundations or among the hundreds of names on the public wall of tombs, or among the names set below simple incense basins. Those names were Bixcul, Toc, Zet, Cuc, Sicajaú, Pop.

"Did you put flowers on the grave?" Isabel asked.

"Yes. I went with your father."

She leaned and kissed him on the cheek.

The three of them circled and turned through this labyrinth of paths between graves and finally came to rest on a slope overlooking a field and family compound. Isabel started again on the school. The grasses below them were an extraordinary green, rich and thick.

"One night, Nina and Blanca argued about how the school was a farce. Nina told us how it was all nothing more than a repetition of the old ways between the three peoples: the Tzutujiles, Quiché, and Cakchiqueles. 'Who helped the Spanish conquer all of us?' she asked us. 'The Cakchiqueles,' she answered. She did not even care if people heard her, Lucas! 'And where are the ladinos making their money here in Atitlán? Where are they putting up their hotels, their restaurants, their places over our ancient lands? Panajachel,' she answered for us. 'Where is the military base that terrorizes the Tzutujiles and kills people of the south shore? Santiago Atitlán,' she exclaimed. 'Do not trust these teachers,' she said to us. 'They are the agents of kinkajous.' She was speaking of our two teachers, Xtah and Xpuch!"

"She's dangerous, Isabel."

"Then she explained that the Cakchiqueles have collaborated first with the Spanish and then with the ladino and now with the foreigners coming into Guatemala. She told us not to be fooled, not to be tricked by the fact that the Cakchiqueles use more traditional clothing than do the Quiché or the Tzutujiles. It is a disguise of their collaboration, she told us."

Lucas scoffed. "That's nonsense!"

"I've never heard so many things! She speaks so strongly, so angrily. I'm not sure if she's telling the truth or if she says things to provoke us. I always feel that she has some plans behind her words. But I don't care. What matters is that she says these things. She says what she wants to say." Isabel again felt her heart beating hard with excitement.

Lucas spun a rock out and down the slope.

"What do you think?"

He turned sideways to her and cast another stone.

"Lucas?"

111

He spoke into the air. "This isn't very good, Isabel. Not at all. This is not at all what I expected. Not at all."

She reached out to cup one of his hands, and sketched a circle around his middle knuckle. "You're like my mother."

His brow furrowed. "Ha, I don't think your mother would be happy."

Isabel let his hand go. "When she gave me the bundle, I thought I was with all my mothers, all my grandmothers, I suddenly—"

"In marriage," he cut in.

She sat at the edge of a grave and spoke slowly. "It is a long cycle of women."

"Women who have found their office! They have found their position and role."

Isabel tugged Marcelina close. She stroked her hair. "Go run down there. Stay close."

Marcelina needed no other encouragement to investigate among the brightly decorated mausoleums with their swooning flowers, their clumps of grass.

Isabel turned to Lucas. "I missed you," she said, spinning completely away from their discussion.

The next day, Lucas and Isabel left the room in the late morning. The woman who owned the room looked at the two of them with displeasure. She did not want to hear anything from them about their marriage. She simply held the flat of her hand out before them to stop an explanation. They walked together to the park where the buses would arrive to take him down the mountain to Panajachel. It was Saturday. The streets were less busy, the air more languorous. They sat quietly together under one of the thatched gazebos and felt the air move around them. When the bus blasted its horn to signal last call, he turned to her and said, "Be careful with those two women."

She remained motionless until the bus was completely out of sight. Instead of turning down the main avenue to the school, she walked around the square, up, not down, and westward to a side street near where Lucas had rented the room. She wanted to walk a street she had not walked before, to discover something, to find herself in a new place.

She walked without much awareness other than with the knowledge that she had not been on this particular street. She listened to her memory of Nina and Blanca arguing, to their outrageous comments, and barely attended to where she walked, so that when she glanced up from her private reverie, she realized in a second that it was a man's intense staring at her that had called her eyes up. It was the tug of his eyes, though she had not known he was staring at her until their glances met. Dressed in ladino clothing, dirty with oil, his face smudged with old dirt, he simply stared at her, from a distance of a block. She stopped, nervously, and waited.

Something familiar in him made her peer closely. Just as she felt that she would remember who this person was, he lifted his hand and waved for her to follow. He slouched and gestured in a secretive wave for her to come, come, that there was no danger, just a little forward. Isabel looked down the street behind her, at the houses and fences along the way, at the brush and ravines. It was daylight. At the end of the street, a couple talked, and a few boys walloped the fences with sticks. The man did not bother to hide himself; he just gestured privately to her so that those others did not need to see. His familiarity nagged at her, and again

113

when she thought she would remember who this man was, he disappeared around the corner. His confidence, her desire to walk the unknown street, the mystery of his identity, all conceived a trust inside her that propelled her forward. She walked down the street and turned the corner, half expecting him to be there waiting to speak with her and to reveal himself. Yet he was already down by the next corner. Isabel stopped and twisted her palm up aggressively. She curled her fingers back into her palm in a gesture to say, "Well, what do you want?"

The man pressed his hands together as if in supplication and bowed humbly. His wave to her said, "Please come. Please. There is no danger."

Within this language of gestures, she took one step forward, but he disappeared around the corner. If there had not been a warm sun on her shoulders, she would have doubled back and gone straight to Santa Teresita. She might have run to the school, following only bright, wide streets full of people who were angry at her for carelessly bumping into them. But the man's evident poverty dissipated that desire. His odd familiarity teased her forward. His pleading gesture warmed something inside her skin.

At the corner she saw him again down by the next street. This time, she would not follow him. She knew instantly that this was a game to lure her on. It had gone too far. He stood in the middle of the narrow dirt road with his arms at his sides. Isabel froze in recognition: He was the soldier in Chuuí Chopaló whom she had seen secretly butchering a cow. Then, he had been dressed like a marauding guerrilla. The image came back of his face crawling with flies, his black eyes peering directly at her in the small cave where she had hidden. She remembered his knife with a dangling thread of the butchered animal. And just as she had caught her breath back then, so she stood breathless with fear now.

He, however, did not come forward. The moment lengthened. Isabel glanced to the sides of the road and at the brush and hedges, the gray and beige of a gravel pit shining through the green. All her fears of the military in Chuuí Chopaló suddenly came back. She did not know whether to run or to stay put. If she ran, he might shoot her. If she stood still, she might be able to talk her way out of trouble. She understood that he had coaxed her into a trap. This thought made her step back, but his hand instantly went up to stop her. She expected a gun, yet he held his hand up to halt her, to tell her not to flee. When she stopped, he again thrust his hand into the air. He came one step forward, his hands out, palms up to indicate that there was no deception. She waited. The man conveyed that she should move forward a bit—his fingers pulling her with small circles before him, as if he were winding a long thread onto his fingertips. She did as he ordered, fearfully, hearing the gravel grind beneath her feet. And then he flagged her to halt with the flat of his hand.

He pointed to the hedges to her right. She glanced quickly and then back at him to see if he would assault her, but he motioned that she was to look—his finger made a quick slash in the air from his right eye to the hedge. She glanced again into the shrubbery, too frightened to see anything clearly. She straightened back up. This time, the man lifted his whole arm and commanded with a severe gesture for her to go near and see. Isabel moved tentatively to the hedge, her hand out to part the leaves, when she saw a body just on the other side of the brush. It was a middle-aged man, marked with blood as if he had been stabbed many times. She spun to look back up the street, but the other man was gone.

Isabel scanned up and down the road, more certain than ever that the military would now appear, and it would be the end for her. Yet there was no motion or activity in either direction. She peered one more time at the body and then backed away to the other side of the road. She wanted to run, yet she thought that running might give soldiers all they needed to blame her for the murder. They might shoot first without concern for her excuses or reasons. Again she glanced up and down the street. Everything was quiet, still. The soldier would have brought his comrades if it was just a matter of finding her close to the body, of placing blame for a murder. Perhaps they did want her to run—it was the normal response. That had to be what they wanted from her. So she moved through the branches to inspect the body. She leaned her way forward through the bush and to the side of the hideously butchered man. When she touched him to see if he was still alive, his warmth shocked her. She lunged back on her feet and ran to the corner and down the next street, where she saw people chatting by a store. She yelled for them to hurry. She screamed that there was a man dying in the ravine, that someone should call for an ambulance.

The people came scrambling. Even the young children came scampering. They followed her to the ravine where the man lay among the debris and gray clay. A man shouted that he would get the ambulance. A woman asked Isabel who the man was. She said that she was only going to the bathroom when she saw him. She was just bending down, doing her business, when his body appeared to her. More people came from the opposite corner. They stood in a tightening circle around the body. A woman called for someone to feel for a pulse. A man said not to touch him at all. Isabel edged back into the circle. She shrank into the arriving people. They pushed past her to get a close look, and in that pressing in, Isabel worked herself out. She did not want to be the one identified as the person who found the body. She did not want to be responsible or to be taken in for questioning. It would be impossible to explain about the man, soldier or not, who lured her into discovering the body. If she gave any hint of a lie, it would go very badly for her.

When the firemen arrived, they forced their way through the dense circle. Isabel had already made herself just another person in an amorphous and expanding crowd. The three firemen turned the body gently over. No one recognized him. It was difficult, with the slashes on his right arm, stab wounds in his abdomen, and two gashes in his throat. Many turned away at the gore. His face was so severely beaten that he seemed pock-marked with disease. His wounds were old enough to be dried except for the slow ooze at his abdomen. Isabel watched only long enough to see one of the firemen push a tube down the man's throat, then clear away the center to free up room for the stretcher.

Eleven

The three officials were men, solemn and unemo-
tional. Their visit was a long and tiresome affair miti-
gated only by Maestra Alom's flamboyant character.

The trainees had hurriedly finished what last-minute
cleaning there was to do and gathered flowers pur-
chased for the occasion into colored cellophane wrap.
These were placed about the courtyard, between the
young women spaced evenly along the apron of the
court. Dressed in their best clothing, the trainees were
to greet the visitors in a united voice and then pretend
a session of classes. They had been told that it was
not to be a formal event, that this was a simple visit
merely to see if all was going well with the program—
nothing to become preoccupied with. They were not to
give flowers or presents to the commissioners. All of
them knew that this meant, of course, that flowers and
presents were to be given, and that it was to be as

formal as their meager conditions would permit, and that they were going to be inspected.

It was customary for a very young girl to give the guests flowers and a kiss. The honor fell to Marcelina, since she was the only young girl who stayed in the dormitory. She wore the Santa Teresita uniform of gray skirt and white blouse. Her hair was tied with a white-and-red ribbon. Marcelina stood beside Isabel with a handful of flowers and a short greeting memorized, wholly uncomfortable in her scratchy outfit.

Soon, Maestra Alom appeared with the three men. They wore dark suits and ties, with shiny black shoes and thin socks. Each had a boutonniere: a small white flower. Maestra Alom carried a ledger in her right hand. They entered as if expecting nothing, as if they were completely surprised and impressed by the over-flow of gratitude that came from the students. It proved to the men how much they were appreciated for having arranged this special training opportunity. The leader clapped his hands together with surprise. He had a face that opened with large gusts of laughter; he held his head back and roared with appreciation. The roof of his mouth glistened pink before them. His belly was large and round, his hands pudgy and short. Sweat trickled along the side of his cheeks. When he lifted a hand to wipe, a gold watchband glinted thickly. The other two men were also large, but they did not strain their poor shirt buttons like the leader. One man had a thin mustache and light skin, the other was clean-shaven with wavy hair. They smiled a great deal, yet spoke little compared to the large man. They entered into the center of the courtyard and looked slowly along the walls at the young women and flowers and at the classrooms behind them. The men smiled judiciously at each of the young women. Maestra Alom then lifted her eyebrows to Xtah, who nudged Marcelina.

Marcelina moved out to the center with the flowers extended. The large man roared with pleasure as he reached down for them. She stood on tiptoe to kiss his sweaty cheek, and then she half closed her eyes to recite, "Distinguished gentlemen of the Commission of Education, we welcome you to Santa Teresita."

The large man rolled his eyes at his companions.

"We are most honored to have here the ones who gave us the opportunity to enter into this wonderful program. We hope that you will find your generosity returned by our proper respect and by our hard work. Welcome to Santa Teresita." And then, in Tzutujil, she said, "We are at your service. Welcome."

The large man again threw back his head and laughed. His buttons strained at their holes. He patted Marcelina's head; he thanked all of them. "We are most happy to be here," he said. "Already my fellow commissioners, Señor Aycinena Neutze and Señor Castillo Abularach, are very impressed by the school. We have come here after visiting several schools, as you know, and this one is the brightest, the most exciting one yet. What a pleasure it is to see all of you, to be a part of this great experiment of our president's. And you should count yourself lucky to have Doña Alom as your headmistress. She is loved and respected throughout the schools in the capital. Now, please, please, let us go about our business."

Maestra Alom led them into one of the classrooms. Xpuch waved her finger to indicate that they were all to follow. The trainees entered and quickly, shyly, settled into their usual seats. Xtah and Xpuch sat side by side at the desk. Maestra Alom and the three men sat awkwardly at the front side. The fat man squirmed in the small chair, unable to get comfortable. Twice Maestra Alom asked if he wanted one of the girls to get him a different chair, but he declined. The legs of his chair trilled as he wiggled.

Xtah began her class where she left off, or nearly so. Instead of continuing with issues of poor funds for even the basic needs of most rural schools, she talked about how the Commission of Education was the invigorating arm of the government, muscled to pull Guatemala out of its poverty and backward history and into the modern age. Soon, all schools would have books, desks, teachers. It was a glorious time for education in the country, and the trainees should feel the honor bestowed upon them as the vanguard of teachers for the next generation of students, some of whom would be the leaders in years to come. In no time at all, Xtah explained, the country would be right alongside the major nations of the world. Guatemala would stand beside the United States or Germany or Spain. Her students would rise out of the small hamlets and villages scattered among the mountains and valleys to offer up their talents for the greater good of Guatemala.

The trainees listened passively.

Isabel still had not told anyone about the body or of the man who led her through the narrow streets to find it. She guessed that the news of the event had not reached the school, for no one had discussed it as they cleaned and prepared for the visitors. She had not had a moment to bring it up, even if she had known how she would do so, or to whom. And as Xtah droned on about the history of education in Guatemala and how the ladino had brought greater wealth to the people, she could not help but worry. She did not know if the man who led her to the ravine was a soldier dressed like a guerrilla, as she had thought since first seeing him in Chuuí Chopaló, or if he was a real guerrilla.

She wondered if she should try to remain hidden or tell everything that she knew. It was one thing to tell the police, another matter to be questioned later by the military. She might say that she was merely walking when she stumbled upon the body. The military would assume this was only part of the truth. They would want to know who the man was, if she told them about him. They would want a thorough description and detailed account. She would have to lie about his butchering the cow in Chuuí Chopaló when he dressed like a guerrilla, or about seeing him later dressed like a soldier, or else she would have to lie in the first place about his leading her to find the body. At some point, she would have to lie and, just at that point, the military would sense it. And they would turn to whatever means necessary to pry open her mouth. It would be easier for her to never tell anyone. To even ask people in the school about her dilemma would implicate them. Yet if she did not say something and it was found out that she was the one to discover the body, they would question her reluctance to come forward. She would be presumed guilty of concealing information. Then the questioning would proceed much more violently, much more painfully.

Blanca fidgeted beside her, her fingers drumming and clutching at each other, her knees aimed inward. Nina sat with her eyelids drooping, her eyes glazed with a faraway vision.

Suddenly, Nina jerked and caught herself from tumbling over in sleep. Isabel chuckled. The other trainees surreptitiously watched Blanca and Nina. Mercifully, the lecture ended in a little over an hour. The chalkboard had names and dates written across it, arrows going from one list to another, and not one of the trainees had taken notes, since the visit required them to be demure, dressed nicely, poised, appreciative.

They were to eat lunch immediately after the class. The trainees all went ahead to prepare the tables. They had taped pink paper tablecloths across the long tables and placed a short table at the T for the visitors and Maestra Alom, who could eat and oversee all the young women, as well as give their speeches.

The fat man, Señor Herrera Luna, sat with Maestra Alom to his right, the other two to his left. Xtah and Xpuch flanked the end of the table. Herrera Luna wrapped his left hand around a water glass and never removed it, though he only drank from it twice. He roared, up there, as the trainees helped serve the chile stew and tortillas, speaking loudly about Maestra Alom's exploits and history at Belén, the Normal School for girls in Guatemala City. The other two men were the audience for all the winks and jabs Señor Herrera included with his old news about their distinguished host, Maestra Alom.

The trainees mostly listened, surprised at the familiarity between Herrera and Alom, but more surprised at Maestra Alom's sudden turn from an eccentric and aloof person to someone with humor and history and foibles. Herrera talked about her smoking and arguing with the principal because women did not smoke. As if on cue, Maestra Alom lit a cigarette and let the smoke fume. Herrera roared and squeezed Maestra Alom's upper arm. This casual chatter continued until they all had a bowl of stew in front of them and the trainees sat staring up at the head table to see when they would be allowed to eat.

Maestra Alom pushed away from the table and stood. "My daughters," she said, "welcome." She jabbed out her cigarette in a broken clay pot. "Today we have with us the distinguished visitors from the Commission of Education. The commission has brought all of us together. For that we are very grateful. Our illustrious president in his astuteness has devised a plan to bring back education to the rural areas of our country. This is an ambitious and glorious idea. Perhaps it was for something after all that the teachers died in the strike."

Herrera looked up with displeasure.

"As part of this program, we have our distinguished visitors, Señor Herrera Luna, Deputy Commissioner of Education, and Señores Aycinena Neutze and Castillo Abularach, assistant deputies of the commission. Please welcome them, my daughters."

The trainees applauded politely.

The fat man rose, water glass in hand, and kissed Maestra Alom on the cheek. She sat down and lit another cigarette. "Señoritas," he said with such pomp that Isabel immediately lost interest. He spoke loudly and with a deep bass voice. His speech was full of promise and hope and great inspiration. Isabel paid attention only to snatches of it, particularly when it became a recitation of facts and figures: "We have stationed trainee programs in eight departments," he said. Nina seemed very interested in his figures.

At the end of the tedious meal, the women lined up in the hallways from the dormitories to the front gate. The three men walked slowly between them all and congratulated each of the women. They shook hands. Maestra Alom walked ahead, her eyes up in the clouds, her black skirt bunching with static at the back of her knees, her mouth pursed over a cigarette.

After cleaning up, the trainees got their chance to walk outside. Maestra Alom smiled at them and said, her eyes remarkably focused on the young women flocked before her, "Enjoy yourselves!"

Blanca was incensed. Immediately upon leaving the gate, she started in. "This proves it," she said. "What lies! I'd never believe I'd say this, but Nina is right. That was pure propaganda. Why are these programs only in the indigenous areas? Why are the ladino areas not included? They have to go through Normal School to get a teacher's certificate, but this program allows us to train without that. Something is very wrong, I say."

"Can you just be quiet for a while?" Nina said. "Let this go for just this afternoon."

Blanca snorted and walked off on her own. Nina looked at Isabel and Marcelina. "I think I'll go back and write letters."

Isabel and Marcelina walked without really thinking of where they would go, but let their feet lead them. Inevitably, they circled around and found themselves on the slope leading up to the abandoned school. They rested by the railing. Off to their right, a female dog with swollen teats led three pups further into the brush. One lagged behind.

They had nothing to say. Marcelina pulled away from her preoccupied sister and went nosing along the rail after a lizard she scared out of hiding. Isabel stared out, thinking of what might happen to her and fearful for Marcelina. She wondered if she should leave as Lucas wanted and return to Chuuí Chopaló. It would be good to see her father and brothers. She might be able to avoid explaining the reason to Lucas since he wanted her to return instead of listening to the corrupting things Blanca and Nina ranted about. This way, too, she would be able to protect Marcelina. Nothing would be lost, except the two hundred quetzales. Yet even that was suspect, according to Nina.

Isabel watched Marcelina poke her way down the slope. She would have to explain to her father why she had returned—that would be the hardest. He would know that something had gone wrong. And she would have to live with the knowing nods from people who would say that she had failed in her opportunity after so much complaining and trouble and pride. Probably she would have to tell the truth to her father. She would not want him to be humiliated.

Isabel watched the lagging puppy sniff the trail after its mother. She thought it far too convenient that she was the one to be led to the stabbed man and that the other man was the one to lead her. It suggested that she was being watched, that he had known her movements, and that he wanted her to be linked with the stabbing. He could easily kill her.

Lost in thought, Isabel did not hear Nina approach.

"A man was found stabbed today," Nina said beside her. She leaned forward on the rail, letting her weight be carried by the boards. Her glance keened out over the lake.

Isabel first thought that Nina was aware of what she had been thinking, knew of her role in the event, but then Isabel controlled herself enough to realize that such news had now to be traveling throughout the town. She stiffened and ventured cautiously, "What happened?"

"A man was found stabbed many times. I think he was left because they thought him dead, but he's still alive, I heard."

"Who did this?"

Nina looked sideways at Isabel as if to say that there was no need to ask such questions. "And who is always responsible? The military."

"How was he found?"

"A woman, they say. A stranger. A Tzutujil, they say."

"They say that?"

Nina looked at Isabel's tense body, her hands gripping the railing until her knuckles whitened. The wind moved the loose hairs away from her braid and flicked them along her cheeks, along her neck, fluttered them across her shoulders and bare arms. "Yes."

Out on the lake, the smallest scar of a wake followed the barely visible boat from Santiago Atitlán. Marcelina moved among the bushes below. She jabbed a stick at something within the branches and leaves. In the compound further below, a dull white sheet flapped on a rope strung between one hut and a tree. Suddenly, Marcelina dashed to another bush and began prodding there. A lizard wiggled out and fled to the protection of another bush. Marcelina followed. Behind them, black birds sheared the air with their call. A soft, roseate smear of light spread out from the wake of the boat.

"I found the body," Isabel said.

Nina looked at Isabel's profile. Isabel had a round face, rounder than most women her age. She was not particularly heavy, though she had large bones and was meaty. Her breasts were large, her neck short. Her long black hair was as thick in its braid as her three fingers. She was not beautiful, but modestly attractive. There was nothing presumptuous in that face, in that body.

127

Isabel turned to face Nina. They stood there for a long moment, staring, delving quietly into the light and shadows within each other's eyes.

"What did you think about the visit today?" Nina asked.

Isabel furrowed her brow. Perhaps Nina had not heard her confession. But that was impossible. Then she understood that Nina wanted to relieve her of anxiety by talking about something absolutely irrelevant, minor, far less dangerous. "I . . . well. It was nice. . . . They were not here so long as . . . I thought. . . . Well, we had nice stew, I think."

"Delicious."

Nina reached out and touched Isabel's shawl. She held a few threads lightly between her thumb and index finger. She raised the hem to her nose and breathed deeply to smell Isabel. "Don't tell anyone," Nina whispered at last. "No one at all."

Isabel opened her mouth to speak, but Nina raised her hand between them. "You've told me enough," she said. "Let this sit with us, this secret, for just a little more time. If you wish to speak later, then I'll listen. My grandmother once told me that you can never take back the water that rushes out from the small break in the dam. It is better to stop it up immediately and then think about how much you may want to let go once you have had time to plan. Then you can reopen that hole or keep it closed, but if the hole is opened right away, all is finished."

They sat up by the railing, watching Marcelina chase her lizard, become occupied with other movements in the grass, hike up her skirt, and pee in the dirt. They watched the colors of the sky and lake and let the wind pass over them. There grew inside Isabel the idea that perhaps this Nina Xbalám was not as bad as she had first thought. They chuckled about the visiting dignitaries. They marveled at Blanca's anger, but mostly they talked about nothing. Isabel wanted to overlook the lake and feel within herself a peace like the one she had felt before finding the body.

Finally, Isabel called, "Marcelina!" Her sister ran up the embankment and allowed Isabel to swat the dust from her *huipil*. "We should go back." Marcelina looked up from the scramble of her sister's arms.

All three moved down the hill together, somberly and slowly, their conversations trivial yet underscored for Isabel by the unknown character of the soldier.

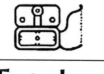

Twelve

Marcelina mewled in sleep and rolled closer to the wall. Isabel arose to go to the bathroom. Blanca lay in bed reading; Nina had gone out to take in the air.

In the dim light of the patio, Isabel saw a large flicker of motion beyond the dining area. She crossed the patio and looked down the hall, past the dimly lit tables and to the ledge facing the field, where Maestra Alom and Nina chatted. At first it seemed odd that Maestra Alom would be awake at this time. It was not late; it was that Isabel had imagined Maestra Alom to be someone who went to bed early. Then she saw that the real oddity was the way the two women spoke with each other. Both sat comfortably together, not hiding or secretive, merely out of earshot and side by side. There was nothing of the exaggerated in Maestra Alom's gestures or any of her strange gazing off into the distance. Neither was she smoking. It was impossible for Isabel to hear what was discussed, and she did not feel right intruding upon them, but it did seem a peculiarly familiar conversation. In that, she felt oddly jealous of Nina. She wanted to sit with Maestra Alom and have a friendly chat, too. Then, just as inappropriately, Isabel felt jealous of Maestra Alom; after all, she was now having a private moment with Nina, just like Isabel had had with her at the abandoned school.

Isabel watched them for a moment more, then crossed over to the bathroom. In the night, the leaves of the trees darkened the patio to its fullest. Light spackled out from under the doorways of the other trainees, and one of the children's high voices worked its way in, but the lack of moon shrouded the open patio with a velvety dark. Isabel entered the bathroom and found Juanita on the other side. They greeted each other. With the divider between the toilets, Isabel saw only Juanita's knees and the tips of her fingers.

Juanita yawned loudly. "I'm tired," she said.

"Me, too."

Juanita finished and said good night.

Isabel returned to the cool air of the patio. Few stars were visible as cirrus clouds glided across the sky. The moon was waning and not yet high enough to smear its cuticle of light. Vucub Kaqix rustled briefly, then settled in the branches. Isabel sat on the lip of the patio and looked out past the dining area hallway. She did not want to be caught spying, but she wanted to look out, to idly watch. She tried to imagine what they would be talking about. Instead, she imagined them asking her to join them.

They didn't. Maestra Alom's arms lifted and fell; her fingers opened and closed, gesturing animatedly. Nina nodded, followed, and gave her own fandango of gestures. At last, Isabel went to the bedroom, where

Blanca lay reading a very thick book in bed. Marcelina ground her teeth in sleep.

Isabel sat on the edge of her bed. "What are you reading?" she whispered. She had already read the title, but asked anyway.

"La Patria del Criollo," Blanca answered, and buried her face back in the pages.

"What's it about?"

"History."

"What does it say?"

Blanca raised her eyes with a deliberate slowness and leveled her gaze at Isabel. She closed the book. "Do you really want to know?"

"Sure." She did not.

"It's about how our history is based on a rule of the Spanish and about the hierarchy of racism since colonial days."

"Do you really want to go to the United States?"

Blanca frowned. "Yes."

"Won't you miss your village?"

"Yes."

"Then why do you want to go?"

"I told you already."

"Tell me again."

"What's the matter with you?"

Isabel stared innocently.

Blanca spoke halfheartedly, as if reciting something from memory. "Because I want to get away from the poverty around us. There aren't enough opportunities for us here. Our lives will be just the same." Isabel's flat expression puzzled Blanca. "Don't you get envious watching foreigners come in and out of our villages with their money and freedom to come and go as they please?"

Isabel merely settled to the floor with the bed frame against her back. Her feet reached just under Blanca's bed.

Blanca sighed. "Well, I do." The book slid on her lap. "I get angry when I see them come with little children who scream and demand or stare at us as if we're in a zoo. They come here and spend more money than our fathers will make in a year. They take pictures of us without asking! They take pieces of us, little parts of us. We've been here a long time, Isabel, and all we get is disrespect. I don't want it anymore."

"You sound like Lucas."

"Then that's good for Lucas."

"And Nina."

Blanca rolled her eyes. "Please."

Isabel grinned. "But what about your duty?"

Blanca shrugged.

"Do we have any duty here?" Isabel asked.

"My duty is to myself, not because of what you might think, but because of my body."

Isabel glared with undisguised confusion.

"My body tells me how to be. All my life I've been separate even when I'm very much a part of others. I'm made to be separate because I'm different, yet everything I've been taught tells me to be one of the community. You don't understand? I mean, my body has cut me away, removed me. Well, I can't change this. If I follow duty, it's following what is meant to be worn more comfortably around the skin of others, not me. My office is elsewhere, Isabel. Do you see?"

She really didn't.

"How can I speak for my village, act for my village, when all my life I've been barely acceptable to it?"

"But you're not really separate."

Blanca smiled knowingly. "Listen to me. There are those who would say that women can't speak for a village simply because our villages are the culture of men. How can we have duty here when we're servants? We're outsiders within our own people. It's only men who can represent. Men who create our duty. Does a foreigner have the right to speak for our village, to have duty to our village?

"Of course not!"

"Well, my skin has made me a foreigner in my own house. Because of this." She held out her arm. "I can't even keep my duty as a wife, Isabel, since no one will marry me. Who will set out to ask for children like me?"

"It can't be passed to children," Nina said from the doorway.

Isabel glanced at Marcelina to see if she had been awakened by the sudden and louder voice. She lay asleep.

"It doesn't matter," Blanca said softly. "You're right, but men will think what they will. They always do."

Nina crossed to her own bed. She stepped over Isabel's outstretched legs and sat with her back against the wall.

Isabel turned eagerly again to Blanca. "I don't understand what you mean about women not representing our villages."

"She means," Nina said with a touch of disdain in her voice, "that women are not the creators of our culture, but they are told to serve it."

"I meant," Blanca said pointedly, "that *some* people think that to speak for a culture, the speaker must be part of that culture. If this is true, if it's to be believed, then perhaps women cannot speak for the people of

Guatemala because women do not have power. Perhaps children cannot speak either. Anyone outside the dominant power is unable to speak for the community except as slaves to it."

"But we're not completely separate," Isabel said. "At least not like foreigners. Or even like children, I think."

Nina leaned forward. "Because women speak to one another and share their mothers' stories as they work?"

"I didn't think of that, but yes. Aren't they making something between them that is only theirs . . . only ours?"

Blanca sighed. "Perhaps. That's why I say *some* people argue that. I'm just not sure, Isabel." Her eyelids dropped tiredly. "All I know is that we're separate, too."

"Can we speak for the ladino culture?" Nina ventured.

Isabel looked up at Nina, who sat with the crucifix above her head. "Perhaps we can understand it and say what we understand of it."

"The thing is," Blanca interjected, "that we are part of ladino culture because they dominate us and change our lives to be like theirs!"

Nina ignored Blanca. "Have you seen foreigners who come to write books about us? Do you see them come and take photographs and ask questions, so they can say they understand the Maya people?"

Isabel recalled Alan Waters and her mother's anger toward this presumptuous American. Her mother had thought the young man nothing but a thief.

Nina persisted. "Don't they have a right to try to understand and then say what they have learned?"

Isabel rubbed the edge of her skirt as if rolling a bead of *masa* between her fingers. "It seems that they do have a right."

Blanca sighed so loudly that Isabel felt embarrassed, stupid.

Nina scooted forward on the bed, her shoulders hunched. Her hands began to move in the air before her, carving out space for her words. "It's a matter of people taking what is not theirs. If we can speak, we should be allowed to speak, not have others speak for us. Can't we talk? Don't we have language? Isn't our speaking good?"

"Yes."

"The Spanish came here and conquered us. They created the ladino out of us, and it is he who has ruled ever since. Now American government and business have come to do the same devouring."

"That's your opinion," Blanca said.

Isabel felt that these two just might be using her as a way to argue without having to directly face each other.

"Our government," Nina continued, "now does all it can to keep the people so afraid that they can take everything from us. All we want is for people to walk unafraid, to go about their business without fear, without concern that they will die or be killed or have their homes and fields taken away. All we want is justice. We cannot have civil patrols enforced upon us. We cannot be made to enter the military and support a system that does us only harm. This is not fair or just. Yet this is what happens when others come to take from us what is not theirs."

Blanca faced Isabel. "Revolutionaries," she said with her eyes sarcastically rolling toward Nina, "say they want to reclaim what is for the people and to cast off foreign influences, but they do so by looking to other foreigners for their principles. They trade American companies for German politics. It is more of the same outside influence." Blanca spoke with a sidelong glance at Nina. "I do not think that Marx is a Mayan name."

"Only the weak will lose their culture during the struggles," Nina said. "Those who are strong will keep it. They will not lose anything. After all, how long have we survived already?"

"But there's the problem of what culture we're talking about and who has control of it," Isabel said. "Ladino or Mayan or male?"

"Furthermore," Blanca countered, "that's what the ladino argues, and the Americans."

Nina shook her head. "They say it while always imposing their will on us. That's the difference."

"Oh, yes," Blanca said sarcastically, "the imposing comes later. Just see what's happened elsewhere with revolutions."

Isabel watched the two of them turn and face each other.

"So you give up?" Nina said. "You go off to be the individual with no cares for your village or family?"

"Perhaps."

"Worse, you want to go to the United States. That's where you want to go! To me, that's worse than giving up."

Blanca crossed her arms.

Isabel waited for the quiet to settle, then she asked, "So how does this relate to women speaking for our people?"

Blanca made an impatient sound in her throat. "I'm going to get air."

Isabel watched her leave. She suddenly felt too small and lifted herself off the floor.

"Never mind her," Nina said.

"I'm sorry. Perhaps I shouldn't ask questions. I'm not sure I understand, anyway."

Nina reached out and they sat side by side on Nina's bed. "What do you want to know?"

"I don't know." She felt a little silly: She didn't know what she didn't know, so how could she ask questions? "I suppose I want to understand."

"About appropriation?"

"That's what it's called?"

"The taking away of what belongs to others? Yes."

"Yes," Isabel said.

"Our people are writing books about us in our own languages. Our people are writing poetry and stories. They've said that the time for others to speak about us is past. We have our own voice. We must use it. We have been forced, since before our grandparents' time, to read about ourselves through the writings of others. It's time for us to do the telling. We need to correct misunderstandings and falseness. We've grown tired of those who come and study us. We're not rocks to be peered at with instruments. We're not stones that can't speak to approve or disapprove of such investigations."

"But what Blanca said is that we, as women, cannot say what our culture is, anyway."

"What will you have Maestra Alom say about our people?"

"What do you mean?"

"She didn't grow up among her people; she grew up in the capital, living among ladinos, cleaning their homes, forgetting. She didn't grow up speaking her language. Is she ladino?"

"Yes."

"She learned Tzutujil and Cakchiquel and Quiché

138

from books and from people who were not members of her family."

"She dresses like a ladino," Isabel said.

"She acts like a ladino," Nina agreed.

"Then she is ladino."

"Yet she knows more about the people than any foreigner. Perhaps she knows more about the people than some of us do. She has our blood. She is both Tzutujil and Cakchiquel. Is she to blame for the acts of her parents? She was torn away even before she was born. Still, she has our blood. Should she say nothing about us?"

"No one has a right to speak for others."

"Yet that is our duty, is it not? When we act alone, we do wrong. That's part of our culture. When we act for all our people, we are doing as we should. Aren't we teachers? How can we presume to speak what is only our thoughts, our ideas? Isn't this the arrogance of the foreigner, who thinks his individual voice is most important? We have been taught that we're part of others. Can we forget our community?"

Isabel twisted uncomfortably on the bed. Her stomach crimped. "So Maestra Alom has no people?" she questioned.

"Should she remain quiet? Should she speak for no one? Teach no one?"

"I don't know."

"I don't know either, but that's what we were talking about. That's what needs to be discussed. By everyone!"

Isabel was now more certain than ever that it was a mistake that she was in the program. Nina and Blanca belonged. They were bright, they nourished thoughts about the world. They read. They knew people in other places. She was nothing but a confused girl from a

139

small hamlet. Her head felt like it was opening so fast that her mind would spill and run into the cracks of the earth. And suddenly Isabel felt tears on her face and realized that she was crying.

Nina hugged her from the side. "What's the matter?" She wiped the wetness from Isabel's face. "Is it Lucas?"

Isabel nodded. "I miss him."

"Will you tell him about the body?"

"I don't know," she said, her mouth wet. Isabel gulped a deep breath and held it for a long moment.

"You did nothing wrong," Nina said firmly. "You don't know anything, so there's nothing to fear."

Isabel took another deep breath. "I'm all right."

"Don't worry."

"I'm fine. I don't know why I cried."

"You're frightened." Nina embraced her again. "That's why you feel like this."

"I should go back to Chuuí Chopaló. I'm not smart enough."

"Listen. Maybe you should wait before you decide."

Isabel suddenly felt the warm and sticky squiggle that meant the beginning of her period. "Oh!" she exclaimed.

"What?"

Isabel dragged out the basket from under her bed. She held up two rags in answer, then hurried to the bathroom. Nina stared from the bed, and Marcelina curled tighter in sleep. Blanca was still out for air.

Chikin

Thirteen

Because nearly three weeks have passed, Isabel begins to imagine that everything will be forgotten about the man she found in the gully. It seems that she will not have to tell anyone, and that her secret will utterly vanish.

She takes greater pleasure in the classes, as if a huge weight has been lifted from her. She loses her guilt for not telling Lucas on his second visit, and then he misses a weekend. She begins to understand a little more what it means to be knowledgeable about things that few in Chuuí Chopaló would consider or care to consider.

One morning, as Blanca and Nina are just at the point of changing guard—Nina growing quiet with the issues and Blanca gaining energy—Maestra Alom surprises everyone by entering. She stands by the door, listening, but the discussion dwindles. Maestra Alom fingers the air to draw Isabel out. At first Isabel does not believe she is being called and looks to her left at

Nina, certain that it is Nina that she wants. Maestra Alom speaks her name, clearly, sonorously, in her deep smoker's voice, and Isabel walks awkwardly out before her classmates.

"I'm sorry," Maestra Alom says. "You must come with me."

Isabel turns to look at her desk.

"Leave your things there. Don't worry."

"Where are we going?"

Maestra Alom stares out as they walk. "It won't be long," she says to the air.

They go past the dormitories and down the hallway to the dining area, right to the gate beside the health center. Two men in military uniforms stand waiting. Isabel stops; she breaks Maestra Alom's stride.

"Be calm," Maestra Alom whispers. "Don't be afraid."

One man has his hand on a cartridge pouch slung on his belt. He carries a pistol in his holster. The other man holds his rifle casually by his side. Their eyes are inexpressive, their faces in slight smiles.

"Isabel Pacay Choy?" the man with the pistol says.

"This is she," Maestra Alom answers.

Isabel nods.

He stretches out his hand and smiles. "I'm very sorry to take you out of the class. It was an emergency. Please forgive me." He takes her hand and warmly shakes it. "I'm Captain Idígoras Fuentes. At your service."

"Good morning," she says.

"This is my sergeant, Pedro Domínguez."

The captain steps forward. "Thank you, Maestra Alom, for bringing her. It won't be long at all. Just some questions, you understand."

143

Isabel stiffens.

"No," he says. "No, no, don't worry. There is nothing to worry about. Nothing at all." His arms stretch wide in the small hallway by the gate. His smile takes in Maestra Alom, then Isabel, then the sergeant. "Oh, this is only a formality. We don't even want to do it, but we must. It is a law, you see. It will take less than a moment. Less than no time at all. I promise. It will seem as if you did not even go."

"I thought you would speak with her here," Maestra Alom says.

"Of course," he answers. "If it were only possible, señora. Oh, our task, then, would be simple—as it should be."

"We cannot," the sergeant says.

The captain raises his palms. "Yet we wish it were possible. It seems hardly worth going all the way to the base simply to turn around and bring her back. You understand."

"There is a room here you can use," Maestra Alom says. She moves closer to Isabel.

"How kind of you. Very kind," he says. The captain pinches the brim of his hat and smiles graciously.

Isabel can barely move. Her ears feel stuffed with pieces of cloth, the sounds and voices seem so dull. The back of her legs, just behind her knees, itch.

"There is no problem in using one of the rooms," Maestra Alom persists. "I will make sure that no one disturbs you. It is already taken care of."

"Thank you. You are very kind." The captain turns his large smile on Isabel. "It is impossible. Now, if you are ready, we can make this very quick trip."

"Marcelina," she says.

"Pwuuw," the captain says. "It won't be long at all."

"I'll watch her," says Maestra Alom.

Isabel stares back. She feels an odd silence winding its way through her body. She knows she should be much more afraid, but she is getting less afraid rather than more. It is as if the responsibility of telling or not telling about everything is suddenly lifted from her. It is now an act already finalized. The presence of these soldiers removes her doubt, her indecision, and places it in their hands—or rather in their questions. She is no longer the one who has to decide. They will extract from her what they want.

"All right, then," the captain says. "If we are ready." He motions to the sergeant, who pushes open the gate for them to pass. "Señora, with your permission."

Maestra Alom nods grimly.

He curves his hand around Isabel's upper arm. "Come, then."

The two women do not say good-bye. Isabel moves numbly beside the captain. The sergeant walks behind.

They go down to the next street and turn up by the video huts. They continue up the hill, past the center two streets away, and turn down a small street. Almost no one remarks or stops as they pass. Isabel sees others notice, but that is all. They walk up another street, near where she found the body, and fear enters her again. She begins to sense that they are not going toward the base at all. Anyway, the base is too far for the three of them to walk to. They should stop to get into a car. This is wrong. Yet they proceed up the hill past the center toward the outskirts of town, always following the smallest streets. On another small street, the tiny fear inside her kicks and turns. She does not speak. Again they turn onto a small, empty street. The distance, the lack of houses and people, fertilizes her dread. At the head of a path across a grassy field she abruptly stops. The sergeant steps on her heel.

"What is it?" the captain demands.

She stares at the dirt at her feet.

"This is only a quick way," he says, his voice encouraging, warm. "We cannot walk all that way by the roads. Come." He pulls her lightly, but she does not move. "Come," he repeats. "You're more concerned than you should be. Come."

They will kill me, she thinks, and that idea makes her want to urinate. She tightens against the urge.

"Come," he says, tugging.

She lets his pull work on her, and again they proceed at an easy pace.

At the other end of the field, they pass onto a small street with thatch-roofed homes. They enter the gate of one and move to the other end of the compound. Isabel walks without thinking. It is the only way to keep the fear from swelling up and tearing through her body.

"Just through here," the captain says. He takes her to yet another gate, into a large home, through a long hallway, out of the compound, and onto a sloping field of dirt heaps and dying shrubs.

An "uh" escapes from her. Her skin dampens with sweat.

Into another compound they go. The labyrinth of their journey ends in a room empty except for two chairs behind a bare desk and a lone chair facing it. The captain sits at the desk. The sergeant takes her to the solitary chair.

Isabel does not want to see anything else in the room. Her one clear thought is that if she sees too much, if she can recognize the surroundings too easily, enough to report where she has been taken, that they will certainly kill her.

"All right," says the captain.

She holds her gaze at the edge of the desk.

He brings out a notepad from a small drawer. "This is just to get some preliminary information. There is nothing to worry about."

The sergeant hovers somewhere behind her. She can hear his weight shifting, the leather and canvas of his uniform rustling and creaking.

"Isabel Pacay Choy. That is correct." His voice does not expect an answer. "From Chuuí Chopaló. Married to Lucas Choy. This year, correct?"

"Yes," she says, but it is not a word, only a cracking sound from her throat. He is already marking things as she speaks.

"Hm. Your father is Alfredo Pacay. Your mother, Manuela Poc Pacay, is deceased. Recently—I'm sorry."

She hears the sergeant resting his rifle against the wall behind her. As the captain reads through his notes, she hears a sharp scratch, which gives her chills; then the acrid smells of cigarette smoke and sulfur enter her nose. She hopes that Maestra Alom will help Marcelina return safely home.

"Does Lucas visit you enough? No, of course not," he answers. "What husband visits enough, eh? And he is so far away, it can never be enough." He scribbles. "Still, it was very good of him to let you come here for the program. Not many men would allow such a thing. He must have saddened his family. It shows a very progressive attitude. Very progressive."

Isabel does not respond.

"Now," he says and scoots the notepad away, "we

147

need to ask some very easy questions. Don't worry. There is nothing to be afraid of." His hands leave the table.

The sergeant approaches from her left and gives the captain a cigarette. He lights it.

"It is very nice in Chuuí Chopaló. I know the place. There is not much trouble over there." The smoke streams toward her. "I said, there is not much trouble over there."

"No," she says.

"You have not seen any trouble over there?"

"No."

"Your husband Lucas . . . he has not seen any trouble?"

"No."

He smokes for a moment. He blows the smoke in her direction as she keeps her eyes fixed. "Everything is 'no' to you," he says softly.

"It is the truth, Captain."

"Oh, I'm sure of it."

She thinks that she will cry.

He pushes back from the desk and crosses his legs at the ankles. "Lucas works?"

"Yes."

"In his family's fields?"

"Yes."

"Is he happy?"

She does not know what to say.

"He is young, strong. Is he happy?"

She forms the usual response with difficulty: "Thanks be to God, he is healthy and strong."

"Yes," he says. The blue smoke drifts to her. "Have you heard that the guerrillas have been stopping traffic on the highways to Atitlán?"

148

"No."

"They stopped traffic ten kilometers before the San Lucas entrance. Did you know that?"

"No."

"They stopped traffic and forced everyone out of their cars to listen to their lies. The people were terrified. The guerrillas had guns. Did you know about that?"

"No."

"No one told you about that?"

"No, Captain. I never heard such things."

He smokes calmly. "Perhaps Lucas has heard about such things."

"I don't know."

"He never speaks to you about them?"

"No."

"He is not progressive enough to speak to his wife of such things, perhaps."

She keeps perfectly still.

"There was a gun battle near Patulul. No one was killed."

"I have not heard anything."

"Has Lucas helped any of these guerrillas?"

"Impossible!"

"Yes, I am sure."

The sergeant shifts close behind her. She can hear his breathing, a tightness in it.

"Do you know who put the letters on the school wall?"

She does not know what he is talking about. He will think she is concealing information.

"Well?"

"Which letters?"

The unseen sergeant blurts, "Are you saying that you have no idea?"

149

Isabel looks hard at her lap, expecting a blow from behind.

"Calmly," the captain says to him. *"Tranquilo."*

The sergeant remains close.

"What he means," the captain says, "is that you do not recall the letters *URNG* on the wall of the school?"

She does remember them. Why is that important? The letters are not uncommon in Sololá. "Yes," she says, "I did see them."

"Are they still there?"

She tries to recall when she last saw them. "I don't know." She squirms. The question is too trivial, like a trick.

The soldier scoffs behind her.

The captain removes his pistol from the holster and places it carefully on the table, close to the edge near her so that she can see it even with her head bowed.

"Do you know who put them there?"

"No."

"Do you know Andrés Xiloj?"

She looks up, uncertain that she has heard correctly. What has he to do with this? Why would they ask about him?

"She does know him!" the soldier exclaims. He moves quickly to the desk and leans over, eagerly. "This is nothing," he spits out to the captain. "Let's kill her."

Isabel moans.

The soldier steps back; he takes the pistol with him.

"Do you know Andrés Xiloj?" the captain asks again.

Isabel cannot keep from crying. "He was my teacher. Only my teacher. All the students know him."

"Did he not join the teachers' strike?"

She speaks through bubbles of sobs, her stomach churning. "I don't know."

"Hah!" the sergeant says.

The captain raises his hand to restrain the sergeant. "Do you hear him? He finds it hard to believe."

"It's true, Captain. I don't know. He was my teacher." She dares not move even to wipe her face. "I haven't seen him for months. Perhaps he did strike . . . I don't know. I was his student—"

"This is stupid!" the sergeant yells. He raises the pistol and places the barrel against her temple.

"You had better tell us the truth," the captain says softly.

Isabel sobs. Words will not form. The sergeant jabs at her temple with the barrel.

"I'm telling the truth. Please . . ."

The captain stands in front of the desk and pulls her face up with his fingers. "Have you seen any of the soldiers who have defected?"

She shuts her eyes.

"Answer me."

The word *no* comes through the saliva in her mouth.

He still holds her face, pinching her chin between his fingers. The gun barrel bumps heavily against her temple.

"Have you been helping these defectors?"

"No," she says. "Please. No. I haven't. Please."

The soldier brings the barrel to rest within the socket of her right eye. He pushes so that it hurts the bulge of her eyelid. It slides against her tears to the bridge of her nose.

"Stop," the captain orders. "Not yet."

The gun pauses against her eye.

The captain speaks softly again, in a quiet, even

voice. "You will go back. We will watch you even when you are not aware of us. And if you speak to anyone of this, you'll be dead. Do you understand?"

Isabel moves her face up and down against the gun. And then it is gone. She doesn't open her eyes and hears the men move, shift, the rifle scrape lightly against the stuccoed wall. The captain grabs her arm and pulls her up from the chair.

As she opens her eyes, a cloth descends over her head. She yelps and instantly feels the soldier muscle her into submission. "Be quiet until we tell you otherwise," he orders.

"Do as he says," the captain warns.

She is moved from the room. The warmth of sunlight falls on her skin. They walk her into shadows and across grass and through bushes. The tall weeds swish at her calves. They do not speak to her or to each other, but pull her from the sides, one of each man's hands on her arms. She feels the cool shade of trees descend upon her. It remains around her as they walk for several minutes; then they stop, still in the cool shade. One hand leaves her arm. The other grips tighter.

"I want you to stand here until you have counted to twenty," the captain whispers. "If you move before then, my sergeant will shoot you."

The other hand releases her. Their boots crunch the ground. She begins to count out loud, her voice barely able to say the numbers because of the fear shuddering through her. When she reaches ten, she no longer hears their footsteps. At sixteen, she feels that she will live. At twenty, she remains still for another private count to twenty. When she removes the cloth sack from her

152

head, she suddenly imagines a bullet striking. But only light bursts into her face.

She sees that she is in a small grove of trees. Far below her, the tall spire of the church rises as a beacon. She immediately heads that way, and her body releases a sudden and cold sweat. She walks against the painful urge to go to the bathroom, not wanting to stop, not wanting to be anywhere near the place she is, but closer to the church, where people will be milling around.

She cannot imagine how she will forget about the man she found in the gully or about what she just endured. But she must push it all out of her mind. Now more than ever, she will not be able to tell anyone. Her secrets will simply have to utterly vanish, like a dream, from her mind.

Fourteen

She returns to the school on that day of questioning just as the morning class is finishing. The other trainees saunter out of the room with Xtah and Xpuch, full of the rumors of her disappearance and of the soldiers, and they press conspiratorially around her in the courtyard. She stands like a trapstick. Her arms hang loosely at her sides, and she does not answer any questions. Finally, Nina pulls her out from the gravity of that center and tells the others to leave her alone. "She'll say what she needs to when it is time," Nina tells everyone. And they part for her.

Nina and Blanca take her to the dormitories, but Isabel turns into the chapel as they pass beside it. They sit in the pew furthest back. Isabel holds her face in her hands and cries. The other two say nothing beside her and stare instead at the Virgin, at the fruits strung high, the cool splash of light on the floor, the plain and whitened altar.

For days, Nina, Blanca, and the other women ask her what happened with the soldiers who came to the school. Isabel remains silent. Too silent. If she had spoken with ease, perhaps with humor or anger, she would have quickly deflected their questioning. "Nothing at all," she could have said. "The soldiers were silly, ridiculous. One man had a crumb of food stuck to his cheek. What fools!" But she says none of this. Instead, she returns with a silence and aloofness, which says much more than Isabel wants to reveal and much more than she dares to form into words. Foremost in her mind is the concern that if she cannot conceal her pain well enough with the trainees, it will be impossible to do so with Lucas. She becomes more wooden with dread of Lucas's visit. It has been two weeks since his last, three since the body was found; she feels uncomfortable for not telling him about the body, and he blames her distance on the corrupting influence of Nina and Blanca. She prefers that to revealing the truth, even when she knows she is forming the first coil of deceit, which will demand another coil and another to cover the first, until she has fashioned a heavy urn of lies to carry on her head for all her life.

Marcelina knows nothing except that her sister is now somber beyond anything she has seen before. She rubs Isabel's arm to comfort her, plays with Isabel's fingers, lifting or spreading them apart, stroking the soft flesh between them to engender some good humor. Yet Isabel remains stiff and heavy. Marcelina takes to draping herself on the bed or over Isabel's lap, usually backward, as if all the energy were sapped from her small body. She falls limply, or rolls like a lifeless form, or sags suddenly down.

"We should go to Chuuí Chopaló," Isabel says one

155

day, after she's had enough of Marcelina's sad draping and of her own relentless brooding. It would be good to see her father . . . to see all of her family. A small part of her knows that she is denying that things have permanently changed. She does not speak of her mother. She never mentions her father to anyone.

Marcelina perks up.

"Lucas will be here on Saturday. Perhaps the next weekend we should go visit."

Marcelina parrots the reply she heard long ago when she asked why they weren't going to be the ones traveling back and forth to Chuuí Chopaló in the first place. "But it will cost twice as much."

"We will need to discuss it with Lucas."

Marcelina livens up for the next two days as they wait for Lucas. The possibility of returning to Chuuí Chopaló, and of putting distance between her and the gruesome events, gives Isabel energy, even though her cramps have begun. This small shift in her, however, draws the attention of the others and makes it easier for them to renew their questions. They want hints.

Blanca, on the other hand, settles into an aggressive disinterest. "I don't want to know anything," she proclaims.

Nina observes.

"Thank you," Isabel answers.

"Better not to know anything and to go about one's business."

"Yes," Isabel says.

At the *pila*, a reservoir with small sections of sloped and rippled stone, the others do not agree. Luci Pac, Angela Sicajá, and María Tun have had enough of contradictory rumors, particularly Angela, who has her own child at the school, and María, whose little girl comes every afternoon from their nearby hamlet.

"Did they ask about the body?" Luci wants to know.

"Yes, but I don't know anything," she lies.

"Weren't you frightened about leaving Marcelina?"

Isabel looks out to the patio where Marcelina follows Vucub Kaqix at a distance. Angela's son squats by the heavy pots and tries to feed rotten lettuce to one of the tortoises.

"Of course she was," Luci says to Angela.

"Did they threaten you?" María asks.

Blanca slaps her clothing against the rippled stone of the laundry rock. "I don't want to hear."

"But what did they want?" Luci persists.

Isabel finishes wringing dry a *huipil* and hangs it on the lines strung across the open area by the patio. "I don't know," she says. "They asked me questions and let me go."

"Then why so secretive?"

Nina stares back at Luci. "Perhaps because nothing happened so that she has nothing to say. Why invent things?"

"Well, I would be frightened about my son," Angela mutters. "That's what I would be frightened about. Imagine, leaving your son, your child. These people!"

Blanca stops her scrubbing. "Don't get Nina started on our government."

The others chuckle.

Nina gives a smart nod. "Yet there it is."

Blanca noisily splashes water on her skirt and slaps the heavy skirt against the rock as if to put an end to the discussion before it really starts.

Nina finishes before the others, as usual, and goes to the room to write letters. Unlike Isabel or Angela, she does not need to wash clothes for family. Blanca and Luci finish soon after and leave. Isabel remains with Angela and María. Those two stare quietly at Isabel as she ferociously scrubs and works the orange soap into an inordinate froth. Isabel stops to look at them, her arms glistening with bubbles. The silence among them speaks about how they, these three, are alike. The others are not. The others do not know what it means to be married, to be with children, or to be already immersed up to the elbows in duties. Just the staring and the soap say this, and the clothing, which flaps and drips like rain beside them.

"They are so strange," María says, and they each know, without having to say so, that it is Blanca and Nina she is talking about.

Isabel smiles awkwardly.

When Lucas arrives on Saturday, he instantly knows something is wrong. He watches her come out of the gate. He looks at her body as they move across the street to sit in the park. His gaze covers her with such a weight that she cannot help but ask him what he is doing.

"What's wrong?" he says.

Of course, she answers, "Nothing."

"Everything you do," he states—"the bend of your elbow, the way your fingers crook, the curve of your shoulders—speaks."

She tells him about the body, but not about the man who led her to it. She tells him about the soldiers, but not the truth about the questioning.

He says, "This is not good at all."

She leaves out her talk with Nina and her concerns about her own life.

158

"Why didn't you tell me earlier?"

"I didn't want to disturb you with it."

He stares openmouthed at her, it is so preposterous.

"It did not seem important. Nothing is going to come of this."

He looks out at the faint mound of Oro Hill at the bottom of Volcán Tolimán. "There is too much danger here."

She stares into her lap.

"If they've come to ask questions, then it's too dangerous here. Who knows what might happen? They may come again. It's better if you return."

Suddenly, Isabel feels alone. She thinks for a moment that this must be what it feels like to be truly an adult, completely responsible for oneself at the same time that one has duties and responsibilities to others in the family. She sees Marcelina playing with two girls from the neighboring homes just inside the black gate of Santa Teresita.

"It is better to leave," Lucas says. He is working out the details in his mind. "The only way is to be in Chuuí Chopaló. Perhaps there the danger will pass by and go somewhere else."

Isabel imagines Nina yelling at him for saying such a thing.

"It doesn't seem that this program was good, after all. It's caused only trouble."

She keeps her attention on the gate of Santa Teresita.

"We can do without the money. We didn't have the money before, so it won't be different. Nothing has been lost."

"There is danger for us no matter where we are," she says too softly.

"What?"

"I said, there is danger for us no matter where we may be."

Lucas makes a sound in his throat. "No doubt they know where we live."

"That's not what I meant."

He eyes her questioningly.

"I mean it's not safe for our people anywhere in the world."

"Perhaps danger will pass by our insignificant home and go elsewhere. Somewhere more deserving."

She cannot believe what he is saying. She gauges him, sees him in new light. "That is a lottery," she growls.

"A lottery?"

"Yes," she says. "To wait and see if problems come or not is to wait for the lottery."

"Is this what you've learned here?"

She reins in her anger.

"It's clear that we should go back. The end has come. There's nothing more for you. We'll act as if nothing happened, and then nothing will happen. That's the only hope we have."

"That's no hope at all."

He cocks his head.

She looks away and across the park at the stone wall of the school where the letters *URNG* are still very clear and emphasized with black outline.

"Perhaps we should pack your things today."

The thought jars her.

"The money saved from the room will be good."

"Just like that?" she says. "Just now? Just today?"

"Yes."

"No!" she yells, surprising both of them. A small

black bird leaps from the brush beside them. Marcelina shouts, "What?" She stands halfway across the street, thinking that they have called to her. Her face is smudged with soot; she holds a pile of earth in her shawl.

"No?" Lucas demands to know.

Isabel looks at his blunt fingers, crooked at his sides. She feels ashamed at her disrespect but even more ashamed at his cowardly desire to flee. She knows he feels weakened and that he is squirming where he sits. Now he will have to act more harshly to save face.

"You must come back with me today."

She sits still.

"Do you hear me?"

"I won't, Lucas, especially if you order me."

As soon as she says it, they both know that it is inevitable that he order her. There is no other way. For an instant, Isabel enjoys the perfect clarity of the moment because surrounding that clarity, or just outside that bubble of clarity and threatening to break in, is strong doubt that she is doing the right thing.

"Go get your belongings."

Her hands fold together.

"Go and tell them that you are leaving."

She crosses her legs.

"Go and tell them that you are finished with the program."

Not even a finger moves, not her face or body.

"Go!" he says.

Her heart pounds in its resolute house.

They both remain immobile and quiet. Finally, Lucas speaks in such a childlike voice that Isabel is certain that he feels he is acting too rashly. "I will tell your father to come and take you back," he says.

161

She whispers into the air between them. "My father won't do it."

Lucas glares out across the park and down the slope at the outline of Oro Hill, rising at the foot of the volcano. He breathes slowly, allowing the anger in him to settle, and, by slow degrees, by slow breaths, he softens. What he sees now is the looming volcano with small Oro Hill at its feet. "All right," he says. It is a voice totally new for him. "Perhaps you'll learn and grow here."

She sits silent as an urn.

"We'll discuss this tomorrow." He does not say goodbye to Marcelina or to Isabel. He leaves, stiffly, thickly.

Isabel watches as he ascends toward the center of Sololá. He disappears behind the jutting wall of the store. She then walks past Marcelina, who stares up the road in his direction. She strides past the classrooms, past the chapel entrance, and around the patio to the bedroom. There, she yanks out the basket from under the bed and rummages through it until she pulls free the yellow letter from the Commission of Education. Nina sits in bed against the wall, watching Isabel's silent and oblivious search through the basket. Isabel leans back on her haunches, yellow letter in hand. She reads it one more time, then crumples it into a ball. It arcs through the air to roll atop the folded clothing. She feels her insides wobble, then reaches into the dark mouth of the basket for her mother's marriage bundle. Isabel lifts up the first small token, turns it in her hand.

"Isabel—" Nina begins.

She yelps with surprise and quickly rolls the token back into the bundle.

"I'm sorry."

Isabel chuckles awkwardly, her heart still racing.

"I frightened you."

"I didn't see you."

Nina cannot keep from looking around the room to see how that could be possible. "Something must be wrong to miss so much in so small a place."

Isabel concentrates for a moment on the insides of her eyelids. She sees swirls of color.

"Lucas wants me to leave the program."

Nina places her paper and pencil aside. Her hands fall softly to her sides.

"I told him about the man. I told him that the soldiers had come to ask me questions."

Nina closes the door. The room is dark as a confessional and as barred from intruders as one. "Do you want to tell me what happened?" she asks.

Isabel looks into Nina's face, reads the lines and small wrinkles, the roughened skin of her face. She sees for the first time that Nina might be five years older than she is. "Why haven't you married?" she asks, suddenly imagining a life for Nina that doesn't exist.

Nina laughs abruptly, stops. She settles on Isabel's bed, her legs straight out. Isabel, still on the floor, affectionately touches Nina's shin.

"I don't know."

"You have no man in your life?"

Nina shrugs.

Isabel puts the bundle back in the basket beside the balled letter, deliberately placing them alongside each other in the basket: the neatly folded bundle and the crushed letter.

"Do you think you'll get married, Nina?"

"I think I speak far too much for men to find me very interesting. I speak too loudly. I think it hurts their ears."

Isabel smiles.

"Anyway, I want to do things besides wash a man's pants and cook food for his family."

Isabel shoves the basket under the bed and sits beside Nina. They hold hands, let the darkness of the room become gentle.

"Aren't you afraid of being like Maestra Alom?"

"What do you mean?"

"Never having known the face of a man."

Now Nina laughs. "What makes you think that's the case?"

"Without marriage?"

Nina warmly presses her shoulder into Isabel's. "I can only speak for myself, yet it seems that a woman like Maestra Alom has had many more experiences in life than you and I can imagine. She's not a simple person."

Isabel sighs. "She's very strange."

"She's very dedicated," Nina says emphatically. "No, I'd like very much to be her. But I'm happy with what I am, don't misunderstand. We must all find our office, no?"

Isabel taps the side of her foot against Nina's and recalls Nina and Maestra Alom speaking together down the hallway. "Was she married?"

"Yes."

"Does she have children?"

"I don't know."

"Do you?"

"No."

"Where is her husband?"

Nina brushes Isabel's hair. "So many questions."

They hear footsteps outside and pause to see if the

door will open. When the steps pass, Nina asks, "Where is Lucas?"

"He'll stay in a room."

"I see."

Isabel sags on the bed. "I think I'm going with him, Nina."

"You'll leave the program?"

"I'm not strong enough."

"I don't believe that," says Nina.

Isabel strokes her in thanks. "Anyway, he wants me to leave with him. It's too dangerous, he says."

"Here, or in Chuuí Chopaló? Or in Santiago Atitlán? Or in Guatemala?"

"I know what you're saying. It's just that I'm not strong enough. I'm just not strong."

"To stay?"

"Perhaps it's not my office. It is not my work to be a teacher. It's my office to be a wife, to care for my children, my husband's children."

Nina takes Isabel's hand into her lap and cradles it with both her hands. "Your strength surprises me. Hasn't it surprised you? It's a strength of silence, of watching and listening. That's real strength, Isabel. That's something to trust in times when you have to fight like mad to find people to trust. It's no little thing!"

"I just don't think I can be like you or Blanca. I'll never be a teacher like Maestra Alom."

"You won't be a teacher like Maestra Alom. You'll be a teacher like Isabel Pacay Choy."

Isabel smirks.

"You've asked me questions, and yet you know how to *not* answer when others ask questions. Isn't that strange? Always there are times when your spirit flags, but one shouldn't doubt so thoroughly the virtues one has proven already. Look at yourself carefully."

Isabel envisions the captain sitting before her, pretending at first to be kind, pretending that the questioning is nothing at all. She recalls his threat if she were to speak. Perhaps she has already said too much to Lucas. Perhaps what she has said is enough for them to kill all her family—though it is barely more than what all of them at the school know: that soldiers came to ask her questions. Only Nina and Lucas know that she found the body.

Suddenly it strikes her as very strange that the soldiers did not ask about the body. They should have asked her. And then she wonders why it has taken so long for her to question this, even when she lied to the others.

"Look to your silence," Nina says. She presses their shoulders together conspiratorially. "That is where your strength is."

Fifteen

It is a sudden and uncommon act, played out in the black of night. And just like that, Santiago Atitlán makes a turn from its long history of oppression. The news of this travels much faster than imaginable across the lake and up the steep mountainside from Panajachel to be heard everywhere in the streets of Sololá. Though the smallest details vary, everyone hears the same story: Early on the previous night, soldiers from the garrison just south of Santiago Atitlán begin a night of vicious revelry. They order people about, smash bottles and property, threaten people, and finally begin attacking local men. The soldiers fire their guns into the air and down the streets. When one young man is wounded, the church bells ring to crack open the night sky. People scatter under the rending of the bells to awaken everyone not already awake and to rouse timid officials. The clappers under the bell skirts swing for more than an hour; at last, thousands of women, men, and children gather in the plaza. From there, three thousand villagers march down the narrow, pitted street to the edge of town and up the road leading past the cemetery and down again to the military base. Their shields are only white flags, rising above them like Holy Week banners. At the base, a frightened soldier fires into the air; the crowd screams so loudly that other soldiers, conditioned far too well or not at all, fire into the unarmed protesters. Eleven people die instantly, the youngest nine years old. Twenty-one others are wounded, with two in critical condition. By morning, fifteen thousand thumbprints and signatures petition for the immediate removal of the garrison and swift punishment for all the soldiers who are responsible. This last brave act is what startles those in Sololá more than anything else. The history of death is altogether too common, but the rising up of people, the gathering together and unifying of demands, the unrivaled lamentations and protest . . . these things give people in Sololá a vision of new possibilities. This rush of hope skims over their bodies, bristles their skin, and travels among them like an unspoken pact as thousands merge on the way into the Sololá plaza.

By late morning, when the people of Sololá gather to hear the officials, the reports vary from thirteen to fourteen killed and up to twenty-five wounded. Reporters from *La Prensa Libre, El Gráfico,* and *Siglo Veintiuno,* too unlucky to be sent to Santiago, wind their way through the agitated crowd to garner what stories they can of the people in the departmental capital. They want to piece together some light for the dark and uncertain future of the whole Atitlán area. The possibilities seem unlimited. More people might be killed in a military show of force and a reclaiming of authority. Santiago

168

could enter into an era of even more cruel occupation by the military, as could the rest of the villages and towns around the lake. Or the base might be removed, taken away as the people demand. Perhaps the presidential elections, the recent cruelties in the teachers' strike, the long history of violence, might persuade the president to take unprecedented actions. The people of Santiago might, after so many years, find themselves free of curfews, of intimidations, of military intrusion.

The small group moving up the hill from Santa Teresita includes Lucas, Marcelina, the other children, and several trainees. Isabel and Lucas have not spoken again about her leaving because the news of the protest instantly outweighs all other concerns. They walk with an awed silence, or with hushed voices, in the current of this sobering news. The streets fill, take on more people, grow like a river with streams running in. Nina cannot stand the slowness; she hurries ahead of the others from Santa Teresita. Blanca walks even more slowly after seeing Nina rush ahead, as if the slope of the hill is now too much for her, the ascent too steep.

Once at the plaza, Nina moves forward to stand with utmost attention placed on the raised kiosk. There the mayor and secretary work their way to the railing to give their addresses. Blanca stays back with Marcelina and Isabel. She remains only long enough to hear the official report and for the mayor to coax free a cheer of hope from the crowd that the military violence has to stop. "These are momentous times!" the mayor calls out, and Blanca turns away.

"Now more than ever," she says to Isabel, "I want to leave Guatemala."

Lucas and Isabel watch her maneuver out of the crowd.

"She is strange," Lucas mutters.

Isabel returns her attention to the mayor and to Nina, who stands closer in front.

He urges the people to understand the seriousness of the actions of their brothers and sisters in Santiago. This is no small thing, he says. It gives hope to all of them. It shows that there is a possibility of protest and that those who died were brave indeed. He says that those heroes must not be forgotten or allowed to die in vain. The mayor, fist up in the air, calls for a march to the base in Sololá to demand action against the soldiers. The crowd hurrahs in support.

Lucas presses closer to Isabel. "I don't know if this is a good idea."

When Isabel faces him, he sees in her eyes something he immediately wishes he had not seen. He feels awkward, uncomfortable with himself. The backs of his legs spasm just behind the knees.

"I'm going," she says, her voice clear and precise, her gaze wounding him again.

When she steps forward with the crowd, he follows. Marcelina tags beside her, yet Isabel demands that she go back to the school. Isabel catches sight of the other children returning with some of the trainees. "Go with them," she orders. "You must hurry."

Only Nina, Isabel, Lucas, and two others from Santa Teresita go with the crowd. And by the time they reach the huge black boot that is the gatehouse of the base, the soldiers inside the startling building have gotten word. Soldiers with rifles stand behind the closed fence. A jeep quilled with radio antennae remains positioned within full view. A man inside the boot holds a phone to his ear. The other two keep their rifles pointed out.

"We want the commandant!" the mayor shouts. "Call him! We want him to speak with us!"

A captain saunters out from behind the boot. A narrow holster bobs at his side. He walks calmly up to the mayor and speaks to him in an unrushed, unflustered voice. His body moves easily, confidently. Only a few of the words float out to those nearest. The mayor shakes his hand; then the captain slips back inside the boot.

"The commandant will come and speak with us!" the mayor announces.

A loud cheer rips through the air.

"The people will have what they ask for!"

And they wait. They wait for nearly an hour. They become anxious and boisterous. Their anger begins to build, to bubble into dangerous accusations against the military. The mayor again speaks with the captain, paces before the gate with his hands at his hips, his head nodding in sharp, hungry pecks.

Finally, the commandant arrives in a small caravan of four jeeps, a blue-and-white banner snapping above each. The mustachioed man with yellow-and-red braids dangling from his epaulets, pins and medals on his chest, silver knots and eagles and stars around his collar places his left foot on the edge of the giant boot. His voice booms out to all of them. "This is our shame," he says, straightaway, without pompous introduction or ceremony. "What these soldiers have done is to break our trust in them, our trust in our own government, our Guatemala. What can we think now that this has happened?" His arms rise and fall dramatically with his words; they yearn for the sky, sink leadenly to point with helpless abandon at the earth. "This is our shame," he repeats. He speaks as if at any moment he will burst out crying from the burden of his position. He is a man understanding the crimes of his dear brothers. "These individuals have acted badly—there is no doubt of this."

"What will you do?" someone concealed by the crowd shouts.

"Yes!" the commandant shouts back. "What will you have me do?"

"Punish them!" others shout.

"Yes!"

"Remove the base!"

"Yes!" he replies. "There will be changes," he reassures them. "They will try these soldiers and punish them for their indecency! You have come here in righteous anger. It is honorable what you ask. It is your right!" The chubby man's braids and medals scamper on his body as he speaks and gestures to all those pooling before the large black boot.

"Can this be right?" Lucas asks, his face twisted into complete bewilderment.

Isabel, however, fairly swoons with the words of the commandant. She hears them and takes them in; the heat of the crowd and the urgency of the situation mark them as true for her, as true in the pockets of her memories, as having an ancient place within her. "Yes," she says, not really answering Lucas or anyone in particular.

"This can't be right," Lucas states. "Nothing will change. It will always be the same. This is a trick."

Nina stands silently nearby, like a mannequin: Her arms hang very flat at her sides; her knees lock together; her eyes level at the commandant.

Isabel looks at the faces intent upon the commandant. All around her are expressive mixtures of surprise,

172

anxious hope, hesitant excitement, doubt. She can see some falling into a new vision, others retreating into old fears.

"Chuuí Chopaló is safe," Lucas says. "Nothing will happen there."

It takes a moment for Isabel to understand he is addressing her.

"The military won't need to go and prove that they have control in Chuuí Chopaló. Not like in Santiago Atitlán. This is just talk, Isabel."

She gapes at him.

"They won't need to prove anything in a village that has not caused trouble."

"Cowered, you mean." She startles even herself.

Lucas grips her arm above the elbow. "This is serious, Isabel." He tugs her closer.

She stares at him as at a stranger. She begins to feel small again, shrinking beside him. She imagines an Isabel who is fleshed out, strong, brimming from every pore because of certainty, able to define herself. "No!" she says.

"This is dangerous," he warns.

The muscles of her arms twitch. She feels herself filling up. "Don't you see?" she says, her ears ringing.

He tacks along his own thoughts. "Perhaps this is better. Perhaps they will be so busy with Santiago that they will forget about . . ." He does not finish and lets the implications hang there between them.

Isabel glances quickly around, sure that others will know that he is referring to the body she found, to the man who led her to it, and to the questioning by the soldiers. A rush of panic shoots through her. She becomes suddenly and strangely afraid that others can read her thoughts. She wants to escape and pulls away from him.

173

She turns and makes her way through the crowd and back on the road into Sololá.

Lucas sees Nina watching them, trying to figure them out.

Isabel makes it to the road and free of the crowd by the time Lucas pulls her around. "What are you doing?"

"Leaving."

"Me?"

She stops struggling.

Lucas studies her face as her mind grapples with its flood of thoughts.

"I am not going back with you," she begins. She sighs, puts her hands over her eyes, and gently, slowly rubs. Her voice changes to a lower, softer timbre. "I can't go back."

He focuses on his fingers clenched into her *huipil*.

"I love you, Lucas."

He lets her go.

"You said that we would do what we needed for me to become a teacher. Oh, I don't know *anything* anymore. I'm working . . ." She stops and squeezes her eyes shut. "Lucas," she begins again, "I want to finish this program." Her eyes open to him. "It won't be much longer." She thinks for a moment that her voice might return to the same voice she had when they spoke in Chuuí Chopaló before they were carried off by the letter he mailed. "When I finish," she continues, "I want to go home and live our life together. With you. I want to see my father and brothers. To pay proper respect to my mother." Isabel cradles his hands. "I want to finish."

Something in him, which is occasionally wise, tells him to be quiet.

"I want to see what happens. Nina says nothing will come of this. Blanca only cares if she can go away. Maybe she'll go to the United States, and there she'll feel comfortable with the *gringos*. Maybe she will find the way to use her white skin. I don't know. I'm confused, but I want to stay, Lucas. I want to stay here until it is finished. Even if it is going to be difficult. Even if it is all false as Nina says."

He looks down at his feet.

"Nothing happened," she says. "That's what we must believe. Nothing. I did not tell you anything. This is the way we have to imagine our lives."

Lucas bites the inside of his mouth.

She sighs again and closes her eyes. "Teaching is the way for me. It is what I can do. Without hiding or—"

A high-pitched sound escapes between Lucas's lips.

She looks hard at him. "Are you mocking me?"

"No." He shakes his head. "No."

"I want to say this."

His fingers weave tightly together.

"I see now what I have been thinking all along. That maybe in one of those children I teach there will be—could be—just one or two who are stronger than I am, one who will be able to go out for all of us."

Lucas smiles softly.

She blushes with her own words, they seem so silly and full of an ignorant hope, but she is compelled to say them just this once, and from then on she will never say them out loud, but simply assert again that she wants to be a teacher and that that will be enough. She will not share her private ideals.

"Perhaps in those young children there will be a sleeping Tecún Umán who will rise up from the mountains of Lake Atitlán to show us what can be done. I want to labor for that child."

Lucas opens his mouth to speak, but she spreads her palm before him. He sees her shy enthusiasm. Yet instead of seeing it as something brand new, he understands that it is more than the events of Santiago Atitlán that have influenced her speaking. It comes from years of Isabel questioning Maestro Xiloj, of her urging Lucas to learn, of her wondering about things of which she has only the barest inkling, of the dangers that live among all the villages of Atitlán, and of the dormant need to rise up and fight for what lies buried in all of them. A sudden welling of emotion overcomes him. He loves her immensely and is ashamed of himself. He thinks that he will always be inadequate for her, that she is larger and stronger and more wonderful than he, mostly because she has the strength to doubt herself and yet come up again, to worry and to act at the same time. She is not afraid, in the end, to imagine herself in new ways.

They walk down the road and into town. As they walk, they encounter people spreading the news of the commandant's words, of the massacre in Santiago. Solalá refills with excitement and dread, with skepticism. At the center, Lucas tells Isabel that he will leave by the eastern shore buses. He will not go to Panajachel and then to Santiago. "It could be dangerous," he says and wants for a moment to do the dangerous thing, to take back his fear.

Isabel nods. She squeezes his finger in her palm.

"It will take much longer."

"You will have to leave early," she says.

"To make it there before night."

"I see."

They sit together on a park bench for the bus: Isabel quiet, Lucas content to learn from the quietness of his wife's body. By the time the bus comes, her hand is in his and their shoulders are pressed warmly together. Isabel watches the bus leave. She waits on the bench for a long time afterward, too, feeling a curious heaviness inside her skin. Her other periods have never felt like this, so she knows that it is not the blood, the water, the aches in her abdomen, but the presence of her self growing larger inside that familiar flesh. She waits on the bench until Nina, returning from the hill, calls out to her. Isabel rises with the certainty of one who has been waiting for just that thing.

"Lucas left?"

"Yes," she answers.

Nina puts her arm over Isabel's shoulder. "You argued?"

"It was fine, really."

"You can tell me."

"I'm fine. Really."

Nina pats her shoulder.

A solitary puppy scampers ahead, looking back at them in fear; then it ducks into a side street.

It is well past the usual lunch hour when the trainees return to Santa Teresita. Everyone settles into chores. They begin cleaning and preparing for lunch. Maestra Alom sits among the young women during the preparations, listening to the chatter about the events in Santiago, watching the young teachers react and question the implications of such a momentous event, of the commandant's speech. She tells them more than once that it will not affect their program. Only good can come of it, she tells them. "These are powerful times," she says, smoke issuing from her.

As they eat, all of them listen to Maestra Alom tell how, ten years earlier, the papers in Guatemala City spread the word about guerrilla activities around Atitlán. Most of the young teachers know the history, but they have never heard it from the perspective of someone in the capital, only from the perspective of those in their own villages. They listen attentively. The Revolutionary Organization of People in Arms had begun to recruit people in Santiago, she explains, and then the military sent in spies dressed like civilians. There were a few disappearances and one or two deaths. ORPA stepped up its recruitment and within the month, the military set up a base of operations. That was the beginning of the long years of violence. The trainees hum in response. Most of them would have been no older than ten or eleven at the time, but they know this small history through hearing it told in their villages. They listen to Maestra Alom explain how every time the guerrillas put their insignia on rocks or spoke to people on the roads, the military attacked innocent people. "It was their way of making sure no one would dare become a part of the guerrillas," Maestra Alom tells them. She scans the young faces before her. "It worked very well, too." She sucks on her cigarette. "The newspapers called it the Ollie North anti-insurgency program."

A few of the young women take turns recounting how they have lost relatives. Some bodies were found and some were disappeared, never to be heard from again. After recounting so many atrocities, none of them speak anymore. They cannot eat, there is so much grief, and they sit recalling in the privacy of their thoughts the years of loss, of violence. The room becomes too dead, too solemn, and Maestra Alom rises to shake away the despair settling like volcanic ash over them.

"Those were heroes," she asserts, "who marched in Santiago. Heroes!" And she leaves.

Throughout it all, Nina sits beside Isabel and Marcelina. Blanca sits apart, already pushing herself away from the grief around her. She should be with them, perhaps arguing with someone, or listening carefully and making facial remarks, but she sits without a word. Only once does she make a soft clucking noise in her throat—when Juanita tells of finding her uncle shot and killed, his chest raw and shredded like hamburger. When Juanita looks at her for commiseration, Blanca buries her attention in her plate.

At the end of lunch, the girls clean up. Most go to their rooms to reflect in private. Isabel stops at the doorway to the room. She rubs her hands across her face in disbelief. "I must do wash," she says. It seems ridiculous to have to do everyday chores or, worse, it seems disrespectful.

"I'll help you," Nina says.

"Lie down and rest," Isabel says to Marcelina.

"Oh, I'll watch her," Nina offers. "Poor Marcelina has almost been forgotten because of all this. She's forever on the side of things, waiting."

Isabel stares with amazement at Nina. "Is that you speaking?"

"Come on, I'll help you do your washing."

"I—"

"We'll both help," Nina says, taking hold of Marcelina's hand. "Yes?"

Marcelina gladly helps. They gather up the wash in the room and go to the *pila*. Marcelina stays close while they lather and soak, but she becomes sleepy and

179

stretches out on the patio tiles. "Not here," Isabel says. "Go to the room."

Marcelina slips through the potted plants of the patio. The old parrot clacks once and dawdles away from her. Neither has interest in the other.

Nina takes up a handful of rags and douses them with water. She looks up. "We're alone."

Isabel does not know what to say to Nina's unexpected kindness with Marcelina and with the wash.

Nina rubs the ball of soap onto the cloth. It is quiet and no one moves within the patio. The others are in their rooms, sleeping or reflecting. For several minutes, all that can be heard is the scrubbing of cloth against cloth, the splashing of water, and the dripping faucet.

Suddenly, Nina turns and asks in a secretive voice, "Did you tell Lucas of the questioning?"

"What?"

"Did you tell him about the soldier?"

Isabel stops with her blouse held in the air. She fights to keep her composure, to believe that Nina is not asking what she seems to be asking. "Yes, I told him about the soldiers."

"What about the soldier?"

Isabel scrapes her knuckle against the rippled stone of the *pila*. "The soldier?"

"Yes."

Isabel hides her shock by adjusting a rag on the line. "Did you?" Nina persists.

Isabel cannot understand why Nina is asking in a voice that makes it all seem perfectly normal. If Nina knows about the soldier, how can she speak in a voice that may as well be asking about the ripeness of a tomato? Isabel tries to remember if she has mentioned

180

the man who led her to the body. She is sure that she hasn't. "What do you mean?"

Nina speaks calmly again, without urgency. "The soldier," she says, "the man," and casually glances behind Isabel to make sure no one else hears.

Isabel feels herself thrown into another jumble of thoughts, doubting again everything that she hears.

"Did you tell the soldiers?" Nina continues. Her fingers stroke the skirt hem into itself to build a lather.

"Tell them what?" Isabel's voice rises uncertainly.

"Tell them about the man."

"Which man?"

Nina squares off. "Not the dead one."

"Which man?" Her mind races to understand what kind of game Nina is playing.

Nina pours water over the lathered skirt and lifts an end for Isabel to take hold. With the clothing twisting between them, draining the water into the *pila*, Nina continues matter-of-factly. "They wanted to know about Lucas, didn't they?"

Isabel lets her end drop.

"They asked you about soldiers who have left the military. You didn't tell them about the soldier then, either. They told you not to say anything." She stares defiantly.

Isabel's stomach sinks. Everything Lucas has warned her about seems to be coming true. He is right. It is dangerous, and the danger can come without any warning, from people close by, people she believes she can trust.

"It's true, isn't it?" She holds out the end for Isabel. "Here."

Isabel dares not speak. She begins to formulate an idea that Nina must be involved with the soldiers to

181

know these things. There is no other way. They have told her everything. She is their spy.

Nina twists the end by herself. "You did very well, you know."

The water drips noisily over the stone.

Standing there with slight bubbles bunching up in the *pila*, Isabel imagines that this is part of the soldiers' test. It is a test to discover what exactly she has shared with Lucas. They want to know how much she has said, or what she will say to Nina, perhaps. That is it: They are testing her to see if she will speak with Nina.

"They didn't ask you about the body," Nina continues. "That wasn't what they were doing."

Isabel nearly gives in to the urge to run, to warn the others. She wants to get Marcelina and flee to a rooming house, but it strikes her that she will be safer in the school than anywhere outside. Outside she will not have witnesses.

"You didn't say anything about it."

In a flash, the image returns of Nina and Maestra Alom speaking privately in the night. Can Maestra Alom also be involved with the army? Are they all spies? All of the trainees? She recalls Catarina sitting very close to María Tun and braiding her hair as they carried on a secret conversation. Perhaps all the women are part of the military. And just as suddenly, the absurdity of that idea takes over.

"That was very good," Nina says. Then she stops and sighs and again extends the skirt to Isabel. "Come on, Isabel," she says. "Help me. I know this is difficult. Listen to me."

Isabel warily accepts the end from Nina and they spread it across the line.

Nina moves close to Isabel while she has her arms up in the air. "I knew you wouldn't tell them anything," she whispers, so close that the words are small baubles clicking by Isabel's ears.

Isabel steps rigidly away and lets the words tumble out of her. "How do you know all this?"

Nina reaches for Isabel's hand, but Isabel draws away as if she will be infected by the merest touch.

"Look," Nina says, "a soldier led you to the body. You found the man stabbed several times and left for dead. He is dead now."

Isabel stands clutching her chest.

"He was an assassin for the military. He was responsible for twenty-eight deaths that I know of. All of his victims were tortured." Nina's voice takes on an edge. "He went so far as to burn a woman's breasts and stomach with metal rods to get her to speak. When he was finished with her, he and his men macheted her arms off and threw the pieces into the ravine. We did not find her head."

Isabel shudders.

"Now he's dead," she says. She begins lathering one of Isabel's rags. "He'll serve as a warning to those who know. The military must know that we are as strong as they are."

"Why are you telling me this?"

She drops the rag and tries again for Isabel's hand. Isabel resists, but then she stretches her right hand out. "Come with me." Nina leads her into the hallway, past the dining area, and into the fields. They sit across the field on a ledge looking back to the squat buildings of the school.

"We'll be able to see everyone from here," Nina explains. She removes a photograph from her shawl and presses it into Isabel's palm. "The *Popol Vuh* says not to take fright over the bones, that one's essence is like one's spittle. It goes on. This is what Blood Girl receives from One Hunter."

It is a photo of Maestra Alom, Andrés Xiloj, the soldier who led her to the body, Nina, and two other men. They are in a garden in the back of a house that can only be in the capital.

"I don't understand." She feels helpless, afraid that everything is a lie, that she is being made fun of in a game that can easily end with her torture. She is certain, however, that she must not show her fear.

"You recognize the soldier?"

Even now, with so much before her, Isabel does not want to admit it. Even when Nina so clearly knows.

Nina smiles kindly. "It doesn't matter. See that man? He was one of Blanca's teachers in San Lucas Tolimán."

"Why are you showing me this?"

"It is a gift." Nina scoots back on the wall ledge. She places her hands beneath her thighs and lets Isabel take as long as she wants to figure things out. "It is a dangerous gift to have, but I give it to you."

Isabel looks closely at the photo. It is Maestro Xiloj. Yet what it means, she cannot guess. Why would the soldier be in a photograph with Maestro Xiloj? Could Xiloj be a spy for the military? Are both of them working for the military? Is Nina also a spy for them? Why would Nina give her such a photograph? More urgently, why is she so important to Nina and to the others? Why would they go through so much trouble to frighten her? She is no Blood Girl, mother to the hero twins who bring the many tribes together. She is no one to be leading rebellions.

"If you want to destroy it, that would be good," Nina says.

Isabel slides the photograph back to her. "I don't want it. Not at all."

Nina pulls a book of matches from her shawl and lights a corner of the photo. She turns it in the air so the flames lick up, catch, blister the faces and bodies of the people. "It was Blanca we were originally interested in," she says, twisting so the flame will not scorch her.

Isabel is struck dumb.

Nina smiles. "It wasn't you at all. We thought she would be someone we could trust. To pass information, to hide"—she rolls the flame away from her fingers—"people if necessary. To keep us informed when possible. We wanted to speak with her." The photo is virtually consumed. "It isn't easy to trust. One has to choose carefully. One has to test trust, as well."

Isabel stares incredulously. "You created a program just to speak with Blanca?"

"Of course not. The program was started by the government. We simply took advantage of it. Whether it failed or not, we would make it work for us. If it weren't for the program here, we would have found some other way. Taking advantage of opportunities is important!"

Isabel tries to imagine herself as a guerrilla, fighting, finding a body like that poor woman's. She cannot see herself in that role. She wonders who it was who imagined her in such a role and worked so hard to fulfill that image.

Nina holds the stiff ashes away from her and flicks her fingers to pulverize the remains. Tiny black flecks drift away on the air. Heavier pieces fall to her feet. She quickly grinds those with her heel.

"I can't," Isabel says.

"Can't?" Nina asks.

"I could never—"

"Wait, Isabel." She drops a crumb of ash and grinds that, too, into the dirt. "There's nothing to worry about. You don't have to do anything. Nothing is asked of you."

And Isabel feels worse, knowing she is incapable of fighting for her people. "But I wish I could!" She rubs her throat. "I wish I could be asked, that I were strong enough!"

Nina pats Isabel's leg. "You are. Andrés thinks you are. And you are. Your strength is just now becoming known to you."

"But I can't . . ." She lets the words drift impotently away.

"You have a great deal of courage," Nina consoles.

Isabel draws back suddenly. "This is not my office!"

"No, of course not."

"Mine is to teach. To watch my children grow. To have children. To spend time with my family."

Nina nods patiently.

"I can't do anything else."

"That's fine," she says. "You do only what you can do. Don't be ashamed or angry. I'm asking nothing of you, no one will ask anything of you. You will teach. That's your job."

"That's what I want."

"That's what you will do best."

"That's all I can do."

Nina puts her hands back under her thighs. She stares across the field and toward the dining area of the school. A tiny flap of ash wavers at her knee, then blows away. "I wanted to teach. But now, my office, as you say, is somewhere else."

"Aren't you a teacher?" As soon as Isabel asks, she realizes that everything she knows about Nina is surely mistaken, and that there is no way to know all of the truth about Nina.

"No," answers Nina flatly.

Isabel looks at the high fence surrounding the field and tries to order her thoughts, to invent a question or questions that will help her understand how the world can have changed so quickly for her.

"Of course," Nina says into the space between them, "now you know that you are safe. Right? There's no danger to you from the men who questioned you. From anyone here."

In fact, Isabel is just coming to understand it: "Those weren't soldiers who questioned me?"

Nina shakes her head.

"He was not a soldier who led me to the man?"

"No."

"I saw him with others in Chuuí Chopaló!" she says.

"Yes."

"But how was——"

"That was one of our first indications."

"Indications?"

Nina gives a curious stare. "What do you think the movement does when it talks to people? Should it come into town and ask for people to sign as if we were the military or we were offering a game of lottery at the fair?"

Isabel grimaces.

"That can't be the way at all. We speak to those who know how to keep silent. We speak only to those who can hear, not to those who can hurt us. If there is

187

a network of trust, there is a possibility of change. We want justice for our people. Like you do. Yet what justice can there be when the military can kill whomever it wants to kill?"

"But why me?"

Nina frowns. "Don't think this is a game. This is no game."

Isabel knows it is silly to think of herself as too important, as if she is crucial to these people.

"Just the information of our existence is what we are giving to you. It's like the photograph, Isabel. It's a gift to you. Why you? Because it turned out that Blanca was not what we thought she was. Instead, you were. We're fighting for justice. You'll have this knowledge. You don't need to do anything with it, except gain strength from it. Strength, as we have seen in Santiago Atitlán, is a thing that slumbers among many, to awaken when it has matured and when it is needed. It is always easy to give up hope; the military has many strategies for breaking the morale of the people. Our way to keep morale strong is to make sure that our strength is known. That the people never forget that we are everywhere, and strong, and that we can get into any place and speak to anyone."

Isabel smiles nervously, with fear and excitement. "I want to be stronger."

"You kept quiet."

Isabel nods. "Yes."

"Now you know me." She stands and rubs her abdomen. "And others. Your strength is not trivial to me, or to others."

Isabel senses in her body the seriousness of that.

"We had better finish the laundry," Nina says.

* * *

Later that night, when most of the women are in bed, or reading or writing, Isabel goes to the restroom to sit. She lets her period flow uninterrupted and tries to calm the noise inside her so that she will understand as well as the rhythms of her body that it is not because she is special that Nina has presented this knowledge to her, but because she is important. All people are important, but no one should think she is special or above others.

As she lets her body be, Nina enters and takes the other toilet. She can see Nina's knees past the divider, just as she saw Juanita's. Neither speaks, though Isabel wants to. Instead, they sit together quietly.

Isabel lets her thoughts river through images: first that she is Xmucané, Mother of the Maya, Former of the Children of Corn. But this is nothing more than arrogance. Because of her pride, she then sees herself as a contemptuous woman with pains and blood and nothing to give at all. Only trouble. Only problems for Lucas, for her mother and father. Only selfishness. This, too, shifts into something close to pride, but not quite that. That rivulet of thought passes, and she travels close to her sense of inferiority. Her thoughts river on. Nina told her to not take fright of the bones, to be like Blood Girl rising up from an ending, from disaster, and into the full light above.

Then, breaking through these emotions and images, Isabel sees Nina's hand appear at the divider, curved upward, with the barest smear of blood dampening her finger. Isabel stares through the darkness at the small sheen. Slowly, she imagines a gesture, a pact—fantastic though it is—and she touches herself. In that sudden and uncommon act, she extends her hand with its own small glistening so that it will be visible to Nina just past the divider.

189

Sixteen

It is a surprise to awaken and find Nina still there with them. Isabel was sure that Nina would rise while the others slept, gather her belongings, and slip away unseen, back into her mysterious life. Instead, she lies there sleeping. She sleeps so long, lost in dreams Isabel dares not even imagine, that Isabel finally shakes her awake.

"You're sleeping too late!"

Nina curls back down. She rubs her face with the side of her fist and growls a rusty, sour yawn of complaint.

"You must get up," Isabel says.

Nina spreads out flat on her back, her arms lazy at her side, smiling like a mischievous child. "It was a good sleep."

"Good dreams?" Isabel asks, with a quick thrill of camaraderie.

Nina chuckles sleepily. Her eyelids are puffy, her

flesh swollen. She cannot stifle another yawn; this one makes her arch and intort her whole body. At the end of that twisting exertion, Nina winds herself back up in the blanket and closes her eyes.

"You'll be late," Isabel says. "Better wake up!"

"No," she mumbles. "I'm too tired."

"No? Come on, everyone is finishing. You've waited too long already. Look, the bathroom is free, I'm sure of it. You can shower."

Nina does not move.

"Do you want me to go see?"

Nina mewls.

"What's wrong with you?"

Marcelina returns from the bathroom and stands at the door. Her face is bright and moist from her washing.

"She's not getting up," Isabel explains.

Marcelina leans against the edge of the bed.

"Wake up!" Isabel says.

Nina yanks the cover over her head.

Marcelina giggles.

"All right," Isabel says with annoyance, "you take care of yourself. I'm getting ready. If you need help, tell me."

When she returns, Nina still has not gotten up. Marcelina finishes changing her clothing, and Blanca has already gone to the dining hall.

"Something must be wrong," Isabel says. "Did she say anything to you?"

"Only that she was tired," Marcelina answers.

"Tired?" Her hands land at her waist. "Tired?"

Marcelina nods.

"This is a joke, isn't it?"

A snort answers her from beneath the cover.

Marcelina giggles again.

"She has to be playing."

The hump in the bed does not move.

"Maybe she's sick?"

"Well, sick or no, I'm going to eat. Come on, Marcelina."

They leave, expecting Nina to come rushing in at any moment. They eat, expecting her to come apologetically. When she doesn't, Isabel tells the others that there has to be something wrong.

Blanca sneers. "We won't have to hear her today. What can be wrong there?"

The other trainees laugh.

Isabel *tsks* them all. "This isn't funny. Perhaps she's sick. Maybe there's something wrong with her. It isn't good to wish harm on others."

Blanca rolls her eyes.

Isabel grasps her sister's hand and marches disgustedly back to the room. Nina is perfectly still in bed, the cover over her head.

"Maybe she's dead," Marcelina says.

And for a brief moment, Isabel thinks that, too. It would have been through poison. She hesitantly lifts the cover. Nina grumbles and makes a feeble grab for the blanket. "All right!" Isabel yells. "This has gone too far. Nina, you must wake up!"

"No," she mutters.

"I don't believe this."

Nina shifts onto her stomach and mumbles a "no" into the mattress.

A small laugh leaks out between Marcelina's fingers.

"You'll be late for class!" Isabel warns.

Nina lies still as a marionette.

"Do you want me to pull you out of bed?"

Nina curls her knees into a ball.

"Go get the others," Isabel orders Marcelina.

"All of them?" she protests.

Isabel jams her fists under her armpits. "Yes! Tell them to come." It is silly. "No. I mean . . . oh, I don't know. Go tell Xtah and Xpuch. Maybe they can help. Tell them there's something wrong with her."

Marcelina goes and returns with the two teachers, Juanita, Luci, and Angela. Blanca drags in behind them. She stands with only her head poking through the doorway into the bedroom.

"Get up!" Xtah says, but Nina is lost.

Isabel shrugs helplessly. "See?"

The others move closer. Together, they all shout, "Get up, Nina!" She rustles slightly like a leaf flicking in the wind.

"Get up!" they shout again.

Her eyes flutter open.

"Wake up!" they say a third time, this time with Blanca, too.

Nina moans. "All right," she complains. "I'm getting up." She drags her knees to the edge of the bed; her feet fall like sticks to the floor.

Most of the women back quickly out, leaving Nina to stand on her own two feet.

"Better hurry," Xtah warns.

Isabel helps her out of the room and to the toilet. "Too late to shower," she says. Marcelina gets tortillas from the kitchen so that Nina will eat as she dresses. They leave the bed unmade and her clothes tossed on the disheveled blanket. Finally, Isabel and Nina hurry to the classroom. Xtah has already begun. They take their seats by Blanca.

"So, you have come," Blanca says sarcastically.

193

Nina smiles back.

Xtah speaks haltingly; she looks at Nina frequently, warily. This is typically when Nina argues loudly and challenges virtually everything that she hears. She usually energizes the morning lessons, and this makes the lessons easier for Xtah. With such heavy silence from Nina, the class turns awkward and boring.

"Are you sure you are all right?" Isabel whispers.

Xtah looks hopefully at them.

Suddenly Nina stands up. "May I be excused?"

"Are you sick?" asks Xtah.

"May I go to the pharmacy, teacher?"

"I can go," says Isabel.

Nina pats Isabel's shoulder. "That's all right. If I may go, teacher . . ."

Xtah nods. Nina leaves, one hand rubbing against the flat of her abdomen.

Xtah resumes her halting lesson. Near the end of the hour, Nina still has not returned, and a flurry of whispers sweeps through them. Her writing tablet and books are on the desk. Her pencil is placed between an eraser and tablet to keep it from rolling onto the floor.

At the break, the trainees cannot help but weave connections between yesterday's events and Nina's lateness. They are already forming the worst scenarios: her death, a serious injury. Xtah and Xpuch don't want this to be taken too far, or it will disrupt them all. They decide that Xpuch will track down Nina. Xtah then calls the women inside to begin the next class early. "Quiet now," she says. "Let's begin."

Xpuch returns within the next hour and motions for Xtah to come out. The others demand to know what she has discovered.

"All right," Xpuch says, and she explains that Nina

194

asked for medicine at the corner pharmacy. Since they didn't have the medicine, they sent her to the pharmacy in front of the movie house. Nina left the first store, but the owners of the second store never saw her.

The trainees buzz with suspicions and theories. They want to go immediately to search for her. They carry on so loudly, and demand so strongly, that Maestra Alom is finally consulted.

"This must be a retaliation," Juanita suggests.

Maestra Alom warns them to stay calm. "It is not good to reach hasty conclusions," she tells them. It will be far worse if they begin with accusations and stir up people without more clear information. Particularly now, she adds, when things can become even more difficult with the officials.

"Continue in the classroom," she says. "All we can do is wait until later today. If she doesn't return, then we'll look into this disappearance. I'll keep you informed."

Reluctantly, they return to the classroom. Isabel marvels at how anxious the others are. Even Blanca is upset. When she overslept, they acted as if they couldn't care less about her, but with the threat of danger, suddenly she becomes a part of them—an emblem of the possibility of harm coming to any of them. The morning sessions end lamely, limping to conclusion until Xtah releases them in frustration.

By the end of lunch, Nina still has not appeared. The trainees go out after cleaning to find out what they can, but they come back with no more to tell than what Xpuch reported hours before. All afternoon, Maestra Alom and the teachers question the trainees about Nina, about how she has been behaving in the past days, about whom she has been seen with, about her moods, her arguments. Xtah and Xpuch search through her belongings. There is nothing in her bag but clothing and a bright blue comb. Isabel, Blanca, and Marcelina watch passively as they sift through everything.

"Perhaps I should have been nicer to her this morning," Blanca says.

"All right!" Maestra Alom declares. Her eyes darken with anger. "You two come with me." She points to Xtah and Isabel. "We're going to find something no matter what, even if we must go and speak at every house in Sololá."

At the gate, Maestra Alom turns to Xtah. "I think you should go down the street from here and ask at the houses. Isabel will help me. We'll go to the pharmacy. I want to hear for myself what the owner says."

Xtah walks briskly to the corner where the houses begin. Maestra Alom waits until Xtah knocks at the first door, then she places a hand on Isabel's forearm. "Lead," she says.

They walk slowly up the street, Maestra Alom very awkward and tentative with her swollen feet crammed in leather shoes. It takes them many minutes just to get to the corner where the movie huts are. At that corner, Maestra Alom twitches her fingers against Isabel's forearm. "Stop."

A patch of shade juts into the street and onto the sidewalk of the pharmacy across from the movie huts.

"She's all right," Maestra Alom says with a heave of her lungs.

Isabel raises her eyebrows. "What?"

Maestra Alom ambles closer to the pharmacy. "Come, help me sit. There, in the shade." She turns back to catch the narrow swatch of shade, which

196

extends into the otherwise brilliant corridor of the street.

Isabel nearly loses her balance helping Maestra Alom lean gently back onto the cement stoop. They settle across from the movie huts. Tattered posters toggle in the breeze, catching the strong sun, reflecting it back. Pasted across one old poster is a flier describing a women's conference in Antigua.

"See there?" Maestra Alom says.

Isabel quickly looks up and down the street, expecting to see Nina sauntering toward them.

"There," she repeats, pointing up at the poster.

Isabel feels uncomfortable having to act as if there is no need to worry about Nina. Yet Maestra Alom seems completely unconcerned and even pulls her cigarettes out from the vault of her cleavage.

Isabel remains patient. "Yes," she says. "I see it."

Maestra Alom lights a cigarette. She acts as if she has not heard Isabel.

"It is a conference for women," Isabel adds.

Maestra Alom closes her eyes and blows smoke. "I suppose one would need to go all the way to Antigua to find out what that is all about."

They sit for many minutes, Maestra Alom smoking with her eyes partially closed, acting as if Isabel does not exist; then she finally starts speaking into the air, deciding a course of action. "In four days, I'll write a letter to Nina's family. Better not to frighten them early." She coughs and swallows. "Then we begin the count of days. In sixteen days—that's a good number. In sixteen days, I will write a letter to the commandant and to the Commissioner of Education. I will send one to our president about the terrible problems in our country when young teachers disappear so easily." She stabs out her cigarette. Only then does she look at Isabel. "The police will come. They will ask questions and write notes. They will investigate."

"I don't mean any disrespect, Maestra Alom, but why are you unconcerned?"

A female dog moves quickly in front of them and down the lane, her heavy teats swaying back and forth, back and forth. She looks this way and that, turning her head and peering into the bushes, down the cross street, into the small ravines, among the cocksfoot, her teats rocking back and forth, back and forth, as she searches for her pups.

"Would you like to walk up to the abandoned school?"

Isabel looks at the old woman's feet. "If you wish, Maestra."

"Help me up, then." She extends her arm straight in front of her.

Isabel grips the old woman's wrist with both her hands. Maestra Alom teeters forward, juggles herself backward like a sweep of black wings, and regains her balance. A sharp laugh erupts from her. "Don't get old," she advises Isabel. She chortles again. "No, go ahead and get old."

She takes a few steps toward the pharmacy, forgetting their direction, stops, turns, and heads down the road to the cross street. They steer toward the abandoned school.

"I spent one third of my life trying to be something I was not. I spent one third of my life trying to get back what I lost. Now I am learning not to try, but to be. Just a servant, that is what I am. But it matters who you serve while you wait for the dawn." She stops in the street to catch her breath. "It doesn't really matter what I am."

Isabel smiles politely.

"You're concerned." The old woman takes another tentative step. "Don't be, really."

"I'm unhappy for Nina's family."

"Ah, so she told you that she really does have family." Maestra Alom ponders that for a moment. "I think Nina worried about her mother and father. Yes. She wouldn't want anything to happen to them. It's better for her to be dead to the world. That's why she usually tells people that she has no family—so no one will bother them. Now, I imagine, she has decided that her family will suffer the grief of a lost daughter, and then they will get on with their lives. They won't have anyone asking about her. They'll be left alone."

Isabel begins to understand.

Maestra Alom glances up the incline past the soccer field and to the hill of the abandoned school. She picks up the weight from her right foot, tests the ground with it again. "Perhaps this is not the time for such a difficult climb. You must be very tired."

"As you wish, Doña Alom."

They turn slowly back.

"I went to that school," Maestra Alom confesses, jerking her hand over her shoulder. "I nearly forgot. When I was very young. Probably your age." She stops again. "Could it be? No!" She giggles embarrassedly. "No, I couldn't have gone to that school. I lived in the capital until much, much later."

"Later than what?" Isabel asks.

"I spent so much time trying not to be Tzutujil," she

says in her distant voice. "Then I tried to be just that. Now . . ."

They continue, and she never finishes her thought. At Santa Teresita, Maestra Alom goes straight to her room and lets the trainees ask Isabel what they learned.

"Nothing," Isabel says. She shakes her head sadly.

Isabel returns to her room, where she pulls the basket from under the mattress. Marcelina enters and sits on the bed. Isabel lifts out the yellow letter, which is balled up like a pellet of grief.

"What's that?" Marcelina asks.

Isabel carefully unfolds it. She begins smoothing it against her stomach. She presses it against her belly and chest and runs the flat of her hand hard over the creases. Marcelina draws close. Isabel uses the stiff spine of her notebook to iron across the wrinkles. The lines relax, let go, and the letter, lightly shadowed with creases, flattens out beneath her ironing book. "See?" she says, holding it out for Marcelina.

Isabel then places the letter beside the wedding bundle, soft and swaddled, and reaches out to embrace Marcelina.